GIFTS OF THE GHOST

The Meowing Medium

MOLLY FITZ

L.A. BORUFF

Editor: Jasmine Jordan

Cover & Graphics Designer: Mallory Rock

Whiskered Mysteries
PO Box 72
Brighton, MI 48116

ABOUT THIS BOOK

I'm Mags McAllister, and my cat is a ghost.

Well, sort of. It's a long story.

All you really need to know is that, thanks to said cat, I can now see the spirits of people long past.

They bring me the mysteries surrounding their death and expect me to solve them. But you can't exactly do a quick Google search to learn more about small-town events that happened more than a century ago.

Apparently you help one wayward specter and more will start appearing at the foot of your bed in the middle of the night. Uh-huh, I'm creeped out, too.

This time, a Victorian-era gentleman named William is in need of my assistance. Now what could he possibly want?

I guess there's only one way to find out…

To our cats:

Schrödinger, Merlin the Magical Fluff, and

Whiskers Montreal,

And also Lemmy, Peach, Lola, and Benson,

. . .because they deserve it.

CHAPTER ONE

"Hello there, my lovely Wax Wonders! For those just joining the livestream, I'm Mags, and we're here at Colonial Candles, my family's candle shop here in Larkhaven, Georgia. I parked at the end of the block and thought you'd like to see my walk into work."

I raised my eyebrows and gave a crooked grin to the viewers. I tried not to move my hands around much as I strolled down the street of Larkhaven, juggling a cell phone and a stack of books. "*Normally* I'd have a candle-making video for you, or maybe a sneak peek behind the curtain to see all the mysteries revealed, or we might talk about ideas for new candles. But…" I said, drawing out the word. "As most of you know, it's only been a week since someone set fire in our shop."

I grimaced into the camera. "Yeah, you heard right. Someone burned down Colonial Candles." I let out a huge sigh. "*Allegedly*. I feel like I'm supposed to say allegedly so I don't get into legal trouble. So for this little story time stream, let's just assume I say 'allegedly' in all the right places. Buckle up, because it's a long story, so make sure that you're following me for future updates."

"Okay, let me get to a few of these questions before I start," I added, tapping the screen to switch my view. "All right, Candy Candelabra asks, 'Who did it?' First off, love your username, but I'm not allowed to answer those questions in public just yet, so you'll have to stick around for that secret."

A car honked as I passed through an intersection, so I turned and waved at one of the customers we'd seen often before the fire.

"Hey, Mary!" I called.

The gaunt, older woman grinned as she leaned out of her car window. "Hey, Mags! Can't wait to visit the new shop! Glad you're rebuilding."

The light turned green and Mary sped away, startling a pair of cardinals off the sidewalk and into the closest tree. I paused as a large truck from the furniture store downtown rumbled by.

"Wow, kind of loud today," I laughed to the viewers.

Whenever I got around to editing the recording of the stream, I would trim out the distractions and turn it into an edited, more cohesive video to post in other social media places. Then I'd add in a YouTube link and a flashing sticker pointing at the follow button to encourage more followers. It made one giant social media network funnel to drive business to my family's company which meant lots of bank if we ever went viral.

I turned back to the live stream. "As some of you know, my family is descended from a Revolutionary War spy. It was one of the reasons that my Aunt Linda named our shop Colonial Candles, though, at the time it was a big secret. Anyway, someone we knew and trusted was behind the arson in our shop. They were trying to keep us from uncovering a set of papers that would have exposed their family for the frauds they are. Don't worry. My aunt and I are fine, but the arsonist set fire to my aunt's house as well."

I scrunched my nose. "*Allegedly.* Now I know some of you have already asked. But please remember that I can't tell you who yet. At least until I'm given the go ahead. So until then, it's a secret for a future vid. I promise I'll keep you updated regularly as things progress, but I feel that there is more to the story that hasn't yet been uncovered. It's why I've been at the library all day researching my family's history."

I smiled as I thought about all the

information I'd be uncovering very soon. Though, I'd probably never be able to share the ghostly reason I'd gotten started unraveling the mystery behind everything in the first place.

"These leather-bound journals," I held them up near my face so my camera could capture them, "may hold the key to the next part of my journey. In the comments, tell me what you think is inside these very special volumes."

I tapped the screen again so I could slow the chat to read more of the comments. Then I waited a few seconds for new ones to populate. "Josie wants to know, 'Are they recipes for a love spell?'"

Well, that had nothing to do with what I'd been talking about, but at least Josie was watching. "I'm fairly certain these journals won't have any love spells, but I'll let you know if I discover something like that while I'm researching. You can bet there will be a video about it."

Another comment rolled in, this time about the candles, not the intrigue. "Oh, Cheryl, I wish I could give you the list of our scents for next season, but we don't know how long it's going to take for repairs. As soon as we know, I'll do another video with all those details. But hey, if you have any suggestions, make sure to leave a comment below." Mary had introduced Cheryl to our little shop way back when we first started.

Almost out of breath from trying to talk, walk, film, and of course, *not trip* onto my face during a live feed, I finally arrived at Jitterbug coffee shop. I wiggled my eyebrows. "Y'all are going to love this shop and the wonderful Laura." With my hands full, I waited half a second for a businesswoman in a pinstriped suit to come out so I could duck inside before the door closed.

"Hey, Laura," I called as I stepped over the threshold and dramatically took a deep breath. "It smells heavenly in here." My eyes adjusted quickly, and I scanned the back of the store.

Laura froze mid-wave when she saw me streaming. With a small squeak, she ducked behind the counter.

"Y'all will love Laura, just let me see if I can find her," I said to the camera while I gestured for her to come out. "Laura, there are some viewers who want to meet you."

"No," she mouthed, keeping mostly hidden behind the pastry counter.

"Come on," I coaxed.

"No," she said, louder this time, and laughter filtered through the other people in the coffee shop.

I fake-sighed, stopped at the cash register, and gave a half-spin, careful to keep Laura out of view. "Well, I guess someone is a little shy today. But this cute little shop is where I get my favorite coffee, and I don't even have to tell her what I want anymore. She just knows."

Laura rolled her eyes before handing me a to-go cup. "Thanks, hon."

Directing my attention back to the live, I held the to-go cup close to my mouth. "If you come to Larkhaven to visit Colonial Candles when we're up and running again, you'll have to stop by and see Laura at Jitterbug. She loves meeting people in person."

"You know I do," Laura called from off camera.

The candle shop was down the street from Jitterbug, and I continued chatting and replying to comments until I arrived at the sidewalk in front of the shop when my new kitty sauntered up and rubbed along my legs.

I raised an eyebrow and leaned closer to the camera. "Now, here is the *true* owner of our shop." Flipping the camera around, I trained it on Shadow. "Her name is Shadow, and somehow, she always shows up wherever I go. Isn't she the cutest?" I crouched down, careful to balance the books and my coffee in one arm/hand.

Shadow put her front paws on my knee, and I was able to give my fans the kitty close-up they wanted. I continued, "Shadow adopted me when we started researching the information about my ancestors."

Couldn't really tell them Shadow had

come with a ghost. Now could I? It wasn't *that* kind of livestream. My ancestor, Maggie McAlister, had come to me as a ghost to help me figure out that my old assistant, Kim, had been trying to kill me and find a set of papers my family had kept hidden for years. Kim's identity wasn't the only one I had to keep under wraps.

Viewers loved pets, so I let the Shadow have her fifteen seconds of fame. When I straightened, Shadow meowed and followed me into the reconstruction zone. I didn't bother changing the camera view. Give the people what they wanted, and right now, they all wanted to see Colonial Candles as it underwent its reconstruction and renovation.

"Ready to see our mess?" I sing-songed.

The door had been propped open by Aunt Linda or maybe a contractor (probably to let fumes of one kind or another escape), so I made my way inside. Stepping over the lumber strewn everywhere,

I strolled through the storefront to give everyone the tour. Aunt Linda glared from the back corner. I guess Shadow was my only willing guest today on the stream. Everyone else had their claws out. With a dramatic sweeping gesture, I showed off the interior. Even though the store had been gutted after the fire, sheets of plastic and tarps hung everywhere, obscuring the source of the cacophony of banging happening in other parts of the building.

The contractor started whistling, a code of sorts to let us know he was working in the bathroom. Had to make sure we didn't walk in and surprise him or vice versa.

I pointed to a few places in the shop. "As you can see, there's quite a lot of damage that needs to be repaired before we can start making candles again. It still smells of smoke in some of the more heavily impacted areas, even in some of the places that weren't heavily burned. It's crazy how smoke gets *everywhere*. And don't get me started on the water from putting the fire out. That's something that gets overlooked a lot. Ah, looks like there's another guess in the comments as to what's in my leather-bound books."

I flipped the camera back to my face so I could react as I read it. "Do the books contain spells and magical ways to enchant our candles to seduce a lover?"

With a giggle, I winked at the camera. "Well, if I had a book that could do that, I probably would be on a beach somewhere being fed grapes and fanned with palm fronds rather than checking on repairs to my favorite candle shop."

Aunt Linda still glowered at me from the back room, unwilling to be on camera, and more than miffed about the time I took to make videos. Maybe she understood *why*, but she sure didn't like it.

Time to shut it off. "Much as I'd love to keep talking with all of you, I have to get to work now. Making things ready for when we can open again. Until then, stay out of trouble, stay safe, and burn bright!"

I'd have to download the video and scrub through it so I could reply to all the comments and questions I missed. At least this would allow my followers to stay updated on how the shop repairs were progressing. Plus, the bit of intrigue with the Kim drama and the secret identity of the arson would help draw viewers.

Aunt Linda thought my videos somehow tainted the family reputation and devalued our candle-making in the process. I thought I'd appeased her when I switched Wax Nation over to something a bit less militant. It was a shame she wouldn't get on board, but it was something I did as much for myself as I did for the shop. I made as much from my instructional videos as I did from working in the candle shop. Sometimes more. Especially while the brick-and-mortar shop wasn't even functional.

Online sales were great, but social media content was even more important when we were currently depending on online sales for important things… like food and mortgage.

Shadow meowed, and I slid my cell into my back pocket so I could pet Shadow properly. "And cat food," I said. "We have to buy cat food, don't we?"

Aunt Linda came out from the rear of the shop. "Oh, good. Now that you've turned that thing off, we can discuss a few things. What do you think about having a new paint color?" She slapped one of those paint swatch things on the closest counter.

Pursing my lips, I considered the options. "Didn't you like the color it was before?"

"Well," she said. "Maybe."

"Maybe?" I echoed.

"What do you think?"

Personally, I didn't see the need to change it, but it was more her shop than mine, even if I did own a half-stake in it. Mostly, I deferred to her. Picking wall colors was a bit like selecting paint for the walls in a beauty shop. We had to be careful. If the wall color made the candles look less appealing, business would go down.

"Is there one that you think will work better with all the candle colors that we make?" I asked.

"Last time, the color before was white with the idea that it would match all the different varieties of candle colors. I'm really leaning toward a mint green or maybe this light peach." She tapped the colors thoughtfully. "Maybe this tan would work as well. It's still neutral, but all of them are a lot less antiseptic."

I hummed. "What if we did each wall in a different color? Then we could do displays for each season and not have to worry about using curtains for props."

The curtains were the reason that our assistant, Kim, had been able to set a wildly spreading fire in the shop. She'd had a plan but having all that cloth and a few candles around had just made it a little easier for her to accomplish.

The whistling came closer and stopped when the contractor stuck his head into the room where we were.

"Hey, ladies. If you could figure out which paint color you'd like, then we can get it ordered."

When we both glared at him, he held up his hands. "Sorry, no rush, but we'll need a decision fairly soon or it'll hold up the schedule. I know you've got a lot riding on your grand reopening, so..." His words trailed away.

I turned to my aunt. "I'm going to leave the final choice up to you. I need to get home and work on some more video content, so I won't fall behind when we get to start work on restocking the shop." I blew her a kiss then scooped Shadow into my arms, adjusting her around the books.

Shadow could easily make her own way home, but I enjoyed having her with me for company.

CHAPTER TWO

When I returned home, I opened the car door and let Shadow out. She jumped from the passenger seat the minute she could. She liked living outside of town as much as I did.

Due to the shop restoration, I had been exiled to do my video work from home. Anything to have a moment alone to get caught up was a welcome relief. Things had been so hectic lately, not to mention downright scary.

Aunt Linda was staying at my place until she could decide what to do about her mostly burned-down home. We had lived together after I'd lost my parents in a fatal car crash, but this was much different. The older I got, the more I appreciated having some quiet time to myself. Not to mention, there wasn't as much room in my home as there had been in her much larger house when I'd lived with her. But, still, she'd be welcome if she needed me. After all Aunt Linda had done for me, it was the least I could offer her.

In all the chaos, I had managed to create a makeshift studio in the small, enclosed porch at the back of my house. So that helped my content creation tremendously, especially with all the natural light.

Shadow waited patiently on the front porch while I unlocked the door and disarmed the alarm.

After the two fires and a couple of break-in attempts, I was more cautious about turning on the alarm system when I left the house. As in, I never forgot anymore. I carefully deposited the big leather-bound books on the dining table and made my way through to my workroom.

The back porch was the only extra space I could use without fear of being interrupted, and I needed to get some content finished or my fans would be unhappy. I sighed and looked around. The room still needed a few extra touches, like a few lights placed, maybe a background or a greenscreen for the optimal video footage. Of course, every time I tried to move something to a new spot, something else was in the way. So I stood back to look over the small space with a critical eye.

My cell rang, and I picked it up without checking the caller id. "Hello?"

"Hey, Mags, did you make it home?" Aunt Linda asked.

"Yes, are things okay at the shop?"

"Oh, fine, good." I frowned. "Have you seen anyone?"

"No…Should I have?"

"Oh, no, never mind. I'll talk to you later." The line went dead.

I stared at my phone screen for a moment. *Weird.* Maybe Aunt Linda was having residual worry from two fires and some break-in attempts. Glancing around, the skin on my neck tingling, I forced a mental shrug and got back to adjusting.

Finally, I crossed my arms. Nothing was going to be perfect, and if I continued to wait for the right setup, then Aunt Linda would be home and want to talk to me. I wouldn't be able to work at all once she had arrived. It was now or never. So I plopped into my chair. After sliding the phone into the tripod, I pushed the record button, and Shadow settled into the doorway to be my live studio audience.

Thirty seconds into the video, the dark sheet I'd thrown over one of the windows fell and changed the lighting of the room. Then the phone rang, but I didn't bother answering.

"Scotch Bonnet," I yelled, startling

Shadow from her perch on the threshold. *Scotch Bonnet* was my own version of a non-cuss word. If this wasn't the right situation for a few almost-bad words, then I didn't want to know how much worse it could get.

It only took a minute to fix things so I could try again, but each time I had to restart, my mood soured a bit more. The phone rang in the middle of my twelfth attempt. Maybe this was a sign that I needed to wait for a different day to do this video. I glanced at the screen.

"Hey, Auntie," I grumbled since I already knew who it was from the caller id. "What do you need?"

She sounded in a much cheerier mood than I was now. "How are things going at home, Mags? Did you get the videos done? You didn't answer when I called the other two times."

"That was you?" I scowled in confusion at her words. So this was her fourth phone call today and the third time she'd asked me about my videos. Something was behind her constant attempts to find things to ask me about. She didn't normally try to check on me this much.

"Oh, yeah, just checking on you. Finish your videos?"

"Working on it. Was that all you called for?" I kept my voice polite, so she didn't think I was trying to get rid of her.

She sighed. "No... Do you know where the invoices are for those new scents we ordered?"

I'd told her this already, yesterday. "I put them with the other bills that need to be paid once the insurance money comes in." I let out a sigh of frustration.

She cleared her throat. "Where did we put *those* exactly?"

"What?" Her question didn't make any sense, but I told her where the invoices should've been. She should've known this. "In the insurance file with all the phone numbers and the agent's card. Remember?"

She rustled for a moment. "Ah, yes, I found them. Thank you, dear." She paused as if hesitating before her next question caught me off guard. "Have you had any visitors lately?" She lowered her voice slightly. "You know, *special* visitors?"

I rocked in one of the porch rockers and tried not to worry about why she'd be asking that. "No, not since we turned those papers into the museum."

The ghost of our relative, Maggie, hadn't seemed to need to appear since there wasn't any immediate danger. Hopefully, she wouldn't, at least, not until I found her burial site and helped her find eternal peace.

"Well, I'll let you get back to work. See you in a bit." Aunt Linda hung up without waiting for me to say bye.

"What I need is a ghost to help me keep things from interrupting me," I muttered under my breath as I started the video again.

Though, there was nothing Maggie could do if she did appear. She didn't impact physical objects easily, and I wasn't even sure she'd show up on camera. Wouldn't that go viral though?

The ghost of a *female* revolutionary war spy.

I almost had the wax just right for the candle video when the doorbell rang. Wax splashed over me, and I winced. It wouldn't burn me, but it didn't exactly feel good, either. Being a chandler, I was used to a bit of hot wax in the same way beekeepers were used to dealing with a stinger or two. I hurried to the door, shaking my hand to cool the wax faster.

Officer Don, the cop who had helped deal with Kim, stood on the other side.

"Are you okay?" he asked with concern and pointed to my hand.

"Burned myself a little when the bell rang." I gave a tight smile as I waved my hand at him.

"Why don't you go put that under some cold water?" He seemed agitated. "I can come in and wait while you take care of it."

"Sure," I chuckled as I held the door open with my elbow so he could enter.

He stepped into the kitchen, following

me like a mother goose. "Do you need some help?" His offer seemed unusual for him. What did he need to tell me? Why was he being so nice? He was always nice, but his voice held an edge of concern under it.

"No, thank you, though," I said with a sigh, peeling the wax off my hand and wrist. I'd never understand why some women paid to have this done to their legs. "Hot wax is a part of doing business when you're in the candle industry. It doesn't even hurt as much as most people think. At least candle wax isn't strong enough to remove hair. Otherwise, I'd have to wax my other hand to even them out."

Ha. Like I would *purposefully* wax anything but my eyebrows. I'd never been brave enough to try anything else.

Where had that thought come from? I was simply trying to delay whatever he was going to tell me. It didn't seem like it was going to be good news.

I took a deep breath and turned toward him, careful to keep my arm in the cold water. "Out with it. Is there something new that's developed?"

There was no point in trying to gently pull off the bandage when his expression was this solemn. It had to be bad.

He shrugged and held his official blue cap in both hands, sort of rotating it between them. A nervous tic I'd noticed of his. "The case against Kim is solid. Unfortunately, the FBI hasn't found anything that can be used against her family. There isn't any evidence to prove that they were involved with your parents' deaths." He looked so apologetic, as if it was his fault that the FBI wasn't progressing as we'd hoped.

"Kim admitted to their involvement. Isn't that enough evidence?" My arm flung water droplets everywhere as I threw my hands up in frustration. "She *confessed*. How much more of a solid form of evidence can they need?"

"She did that in private. There wasn't a recording. For some reason, nothing of the confession was taped and can't be used against the family. And even then, she confessed that someone else committed a crime. And that supposed criminal is dead." He shrugged as if waiting for another outburst from me.

"It's not your fault," I sighed in resignation. He had nothing to do with the cameras or if they were recorded properly. Don would've done anything to keep this case moving. "Thanks for telling me."

Well, Scotch Bonnet. This just stinks. I slammed my hand on the counter, sending a tingle through the sensitive skin. Now what?

CHAPTER THREE

Don tucked his hat beneath his arm, grabbed the dish towel from the oven, and handed it to me to dry my hands as I fumed at the turn of events.

"Look, I'm really sorry," he said as I took the towel. He stood there with his hands on his hat as if he wasn't certain about what to do with himself. "If you'd like a ride to your next court date, I could pick you up. They want you to testify, right?

"I have a car," I said, wetting the dish towel and dabbing it on my hand to clear off any remaining wax droplets.

He cleared his throat. "Well, this way, y 'know, you wouldn't have to go alone."

"Oh." It would be nice to have someone there on my team since I was nervous about the whole thing. "The lawyers have asked me to testify," I said, finally freeing myself from my train of thought. "I don't want to." My hands twisted nervously at the idea, wringing the dishtowel nearly into a knot. "I know that it's what I *need* to do, but that doesn't make it any easier."

He laid a comforting hand on my shoulder. "It's your choice, of course. If you can, then it will go a long way to convincing the judge that she's guilty. They'll need your testimony to make the conviction stick."

Aggravated, I paced back and forth in the small space. "Is it even worth going to all this trouble if the people who killed my parents aren't punished for what they did?"

"Kim needs to be punished for what she did."

"At least they didn't kill Aunt Linda."

I sighed, but then it hit me. "I guess Kim almost *did* kill her. That's way too close to losing my parents all over again."

"Look, no pressure," Don said, wringing his cap in his hands. "We don't have to go together. I just thought that if I could be there to lend some support and help you through the process that it might be easier for you." He shrugged as if it wasn't really that big of a deal.

My brain flew to Wes, my British viscount veterinary crush. He'd been MIA since he'd gotten back from an out-of-town work conference. I'd made a few excuses about him having to catch up on work at his veterinary practice in Larkhaven, but I wanted him to be at the trial as well.

Maybe I had just imagined that he was okay with everything making its way into the public eye. As a member of the Howe family, he might have been more bothered by the documents that I'd released than he'd let on.

Don had been around during all the chaos. He'd honestly made me feel safe and had been a great help as my life slowly fell apart. And that counted for something, didn't it?

"Yes." I let out like a breath I'd been holding. I just needed to give him an answer before I could think too much about it. "I'd really like that since Aunt Linda can't be there with me while I'm testifying."

"That is, if you're sure that won't be too much trouble," I hastened to add. "I wouldn't want you skipping work on my account."

A half-restrained chuckle shook his chest as a smile broke out across his face. "Not at all. I'd love to be there for you."

He nodded toward the towel that I'd unconsciously wrapped around my arm and part of my hand. "How's your burn doing?"

"Huh," I said absently, unwinding the towel. "The stinging isn't bad, but… Huh." I stared at a few raised welts where the wax had been the hottest. I'd never been burned by wax quite like that before. "I'll need to check my temperatures. It shouldn't have been hot enough to cause a blister. At least not like that."

He grimaced at my arm. "Doesn't look bad enough to need a doctor, though. Do you have any burn cream?"

I grinned. "In my line of work, I'd be stupid not to have some in the house."

"Do you want me to get it?"

"No, I can do that. It takes more than a little burn to stop me."

He chuckled and put his hat back on. "Now that's some truth." He stopped mid-turn and glanced back at me. "Should I pick you up about an hour before we have to be there?"

I tipped my head to the side and smiled. It was nice to be thought of like that, and I appreciated it more than he probably knew. "That would be perfect. Thank you for being willing to lend my support for this. Not everybody would be willing to do that."

"Anytime," he chuffed, with an almost sauntering step toward the living room. "I should probably skedaddle. I'm technically on duty right now."

"I'll see you out." I felt a little better about the trial. It was going to be bearable now. At least I'd have a friend rooting for me.

As I closed the front door behind him and turned back toward the kitchen, I spotted Shadow sitting on the table next to the sink. Maggie stood beside her. *Oh, no.* I hadn't seen Maggie in a while, and her turning up again wasn't necessarily a good thing.

She gestured toward my cell phone, sitting on the counter. It had been far enough out of the mess I'd made while flinging my wet hands around that it hadn't gotten ruined.

I jogged toward it and picked it up. An email from the fire inspector. The blaze was definitely arson. They had definitive proof and everything they needed to make the case against Kim stick.

There was another email right after that one, and it was from the company securing the stairs to the attic. Aunt Linda's attic hadn't burned in the fire.

While the rest of the house had been practically destroyed, the attic hadn't been as badly damaged, so the remaining structure had been rebuilt enough for us to retrieve whatever important items we could from up there.

The email also contained an invoice and an estimate of when the project was supposed to be stable enough for me to hike up the stairs. They were certain that it would be safe within a week.

Questions brimmed on the tip of my tongue for Maggie as I looked up, only to find her gone.

I shook my head at her vanishing act. If only I could've found proof of who killed Maggie, then I could've found her body. Maybe finding her body would have released her from being trapped in Larkhaven.

Shadow hopped up onto the counter and allowed me to scratch her behind the ears as I reread the emails and thought about what was coming.

All my video content wasn't going to make itself, so I went back into my overflowing workspace to see what I could do with the time I had left. With only a few more hiccups, I was able to produce a few videos that I'd be able to upload and schedule for posting, which I desperately needed so I could stay relevant and visible.

The phone rang, and for a fleeting moment, I hoped it might be Wes. But no such luck. Caller ID said it was Aunt Linda calling, yet again. Not that I minded, but I couldn't help wondering where Wes was and what he was doing. I missed him.

"Hello?"

"Mags, I can't find those jars we ordered for the new scents." Aunt Linda sounded frazzled.

"Oh, those should still be in boxes in the back room." Why couldn't she find anything lately? I was going to have to put her on a multivitamin.

"Any visitors?" Aunt Linda asked again.

I rolled my eyes, but Don had come by, and she'd probably want to hear about what he'd said. "Well, funny thing. Don, the cop, dropped by. He said that Kim's confession didn't get taped." I frowned, stamping down a burst of fury at the problem. I unfolded and re-folded the wet towel I'd used earlier. How had they messed up the recording? One button. That's all anybody had to push. They did this for a living. How did— *No.* I brought that train of thought to a screeching halt since it wasn't helpful.

Aunt Linda sighed. "He mentioned that when he came by earlier. He thought you could use someone to be there for you at the hearing." She waited for me to protest. When I didn't, she added, "He's a nice young man. I think he's sweet on you."

Ah, so that was why she'd called approximately fifty-seven times since I got home. "Thanks, Auntie, I already told him he could take me if it wasn't too much of a bother."

"Why would you be a bother?" She dismissed my concern. "He's not going to think that when he wants you to like him. It's how dating works."

Dating? She thought we were dating. I continued to fold and refold the towel again and again until I remembered the email from the repair company for the house. "The structural company sent a notice telling us that the stairs should be safe to go in the attic soon."

"Don't you think that we should just hire someone to tear the whole place down? Is it really going to be safe for us to be there after all that's happened?" Aunt Linda suddenly sounded tired.

I looked down at the towel, not really paying attention to much except the weariness in Aunt Linda's words. When I glanced up, Maggie was standing next to me, appearing distressed and shaking her head no.

Maggie didn't want anyone tearing down the attic or messing with our family history. Not that I blamed her one little bit. It felt totally wrong to me, too. I studied Maggie's expression. Who knew a ghost could have such an expressive face?

"Mags? Are you still there?"

"Oh, um, I don't think anyone else should go up there except for you or me. It doesn't feel right."

"Fine. If you think so. We just need to make sure that you're safe when you go up the stairs," she cautioned. "I can't have anything happen to you."

"It'll be okay, Auntie," I promised. "Besides, I want to look around up there for clues about Maggie's ghost, and I'm sure there's all kinds of important stuff up there."

"Well, don't be disappointed if you don't find anything. Either way, dear, I'll be home in a little bit."

"Be safe, Auntie. See you soon."

CHAPTER FOUR

The next day, I got up bright and early, ready to start working on more content. While it was true that I should've been doing videos, I missed all my book club people. Aunt Linda had been working up at the shop a lot more lately since things needed to be ready to reopen and the shop was *her* baby. Once upon a time, the book club had been mine.

Maybe I could summon my bookish friends on a whim. I sent out a barrage of texts, requesting a book club meeting later in the day, and with enough enthusiastic replies, we were able to schedule an impromptu meeting.

After a shower and breakfast, I sat down to plan what videos to make next. More dipping, of course. Those were always popular and led people to our shop. Maybe some footage of the burned-out house. They'd like to see that, and I could talk about the repairs.

I had more followers now than I did only a few months ago. It was more important than ever that I make up for the lost revenue from the shop with social media content. However much Aunt Linda disliked it, it was currently saving our bacon. But the harder I tried to focus on making videos, the more my mind wandered to my book club friends. Since I wasn't getting any work done at home, I decided to head into the shop.

So I grabbed my phone, purse, and key fob to head into town. If nothing else, I needed coffee. The radio was on, and I hummed along to the song playing. As I glanced behind me, I noticed a car following much closer than was normal in a place like Larkhaven.

I mashed on the gas pedal and sped up, but the car behind me maintained the same speed as I did. Town was rapidly approaching, but I was anxious that the car was still following me.

Just as I was about to try the turn right three times trick to try to lose them, the sound of sirens filled the air. I pulled the car to the side of the road as fire trucks and police cars raced by. Distracted by the emergency vehicles, I lost sight of the other car from my rearview.

Maybe I was being paranoid. My heart pounded in my chest, and I wiped my sweaty palms against the steering wheel. I was probably overreacting, right?

But I had a reason, didn't I? It hadn't been that long since someone had tried to hurt us. The buildings still reeked of smoke.

However, Kim was in jail. She couldn't hurt me now. She was behind bars. It couldn't be her, and the ghosts of her family didn't drive cars. That knowledge was the only thing that calmed me down.

When I pulled back onto the highway, I made it to town without further incident.

I studied my surroundings as I pulled into the shop parking lot, looking for anything that seemed suspicious. Still nervous, I didn't see anyone watching me or paying special attention to my actions. Everything appeared normal for our small town. With a deep breath, I hopped out of my car and did my best impression of someone that wasn't a Paranoid Patty.

That quickly failed when Shadow trotted alongside my legs, causing me to jump. I shook it off with a chuckle as I hurried into the shop. "Hey, girl, decided not to stay home?"

I had no idea how she got to the shop from home or back so quickly. It had to be something to do with her showing up when Maggie the ghost had. Maybe

Shadow had paranormal skills, too. I hadn't brought her with me, that much I knew. Yet here she was.

The bell on the front door chimed, and Aunt Linda glanced up from where she was working on something behind the counter. She waved. "You were sleeping when I left."

"I guess I was tired." Unease filled me, and I liked to stay busy when I was nervous. I chewed my bottom lip, trying to decide which project to tackle first. "We've had a lot happening," I muttered to myself.

"What's going on?" Aunt Linda asked. "You're not your normal chipper self."

"I'm just a bit jittery. Thought I'd been followed by another car, but then I remembered that Kim was in jail."

"Oh, maybe we should find somebody for you to talk to, or maybe you need some time off?"

"Not right now. I'm fine. See? It's already going away." Waving her off, I carried on straightening shelves that would likely get messed up again as the construction workers continued their efforts. But setting the shelves right helped calm me. There was something calming about bringing order to chaos. "Besides, you're the one who needs time off, Auntie."

"Oh, honey," Aunt Linda sympathized with a smile. "You know I can't do that." She drummed her fingers on the counter. "Though, that does bring up another subject that we need to talk about: hiring a replacement."

A flood of negative feelings threatened to overwhelm me. I had trusted Kim. She'd been a close friend, and she'd tried to burn down our homes and our livelihood. I wasn't sure we were ready to bring someone else into the shop so soon after almost losing our lives.

Aunt Linda must have sensed the growing tension inside me. "We can't do it all alone. At some point, we'll have to hire someone. Better to go ahead and rip that band-aid off now, than to let it continue to worry us."

I sighed. As much as I didn't like it, she was right. "There are a lot of online orders with the shop being closed for renovations. That would at least give a new employee something we could train them on. I guess we can see if there's someone that might work out."

My phone alarm jangled to alert me that it was time to head over to the Jitterbug for our book club meeting.

"I'm going to book club. See you at home, Auntie," I called as I headed out the door. I was taking an hour for myself. Something I'd barely done in the last few weeks.

The others were all sitting at one of the tables drinking coffee when I arrived, slightly out of breath. "Hi, everyone."

Laura and Lacy both jumped up and embraced me. Extracting myself from their hug, I returned smiles to the other members as I took a seat at the table with them.

"I'm so glad that you suggested this," Lacy whispered as she hugged me. "It's time we got back to our normal routines."

Happiness filled me, and the sense of paranoia fled. "What are we reading today?"

CHAPTER FIVE

The morning of the trial had arrived. It had only been a week since Don had asked to accompany me to testify. I'd spent it making videos, helping at the shop, and trying not to be completely nervous about court.

Shadow followed me from room to room as I tried to get ready. With how attentive she'd been, I kept expecting to see Maggie pop up as they seemed to be connected. But Maggie hadn't appeared since she'd told me to check my emails.

Rough was the only word for how my morning had gone so far. The coffee had gone down the front of my shirt instead of into my mouth. My hair had refused to cooperate, and I'd sneezed in the middle of trying to do eyeliner and got wild with the mascara wand on the follow-up, so I'd had to redo my makeup *twice.*

The new shoes I'd been saving for a special occasion pinched my toes. I regretted not taking the time to break them in before wearing them to the trial. None of the other pairs would work with the outfit I had chosen, the most professional look in my closet. Besides, my current look had been pressed. Half of everything else had wax bits or dye splatters and everything else needed to take their turn at the dry cleaners.

And now the sleeves of the outfit I'd chosen didn't cover the last bit of burn on my arm. Instead, it felt like everyone in the courtroom would be staring at the wax burn on the chandler's arm.

Dread had been growing in the pit of my stomach with each new problem, and everything was going wrong this morning. Was this a series of omens, telling me testifying was a terrible idea?

I shrugged as the doorbell sounded. Not much I could do to change things now. I'd agreed to do it, and my ride was here.

Rather than his usual work uniform, Don stood dressed in a smart blue suit when I opened the door. His shoulders filled the jacket, and the trousers hugged his waist. He looked so handsome, and his relaxed grin helped relieve some of the butterflies in my stomach.

"Hey there." Don beamed at me, but he didn't come inside. His expression turned more solemn. "Are you ready for this?"

"Yes," I answered automatically, even though I was anything but ready.

The corners of his mouth tipped down, and his gaze narrowed. "You look a little like you need one of those little bags from the airplane. You know which ones I mean?"

"I'm not used to this," I said. He was trying to make a joke, but it didn't help.

"Oh, you'll do well, Mags," he said. "And you look amazing."

I rolled my shoulders to release some of the tension. Then I noticed that Maggie hovered right behind him on the porch. She was solemn, and I couldn't help worrying that something was wrong. She rarely turned up unless she thought I needed help. And she was usually right. Whatever stress I'd managed to dispel snapped right back.

"Let's get this over with," I said, grabbing my coat and purse from the entryway before locking the door and setting the alarm.

Don escorted me to his truck, doing his best to give me space, but his closeness let me know he was here for me if I needed him.

We rode in silence, which felt comfortable, not awkward. His radio played, but the volume was so low I couldn't make out any lyrics or even the music. There wasn't a need to chatter away, but as we got closer to the courthouse, the more doubt began to creep into my mind.

"How do you think the case is going to go?" I twisted my hands in my lap, nervous I was going to mess things up. "I've never been questioned before. Shoot, I've never even been on a jury before."

"Most people haven't had to testify before." He chuckled. "Movies make it seem really intense and like there's going to be this big emotional roller coaster. It's not. It won't be nearly as bad as you've imagined it to be. You aren't the person on trial. They're using your testimony to establish a full record of what's happened. They'll ask some questions to be certain your statement is the truth. It's to clarify any small details that are needed to assure that Kim is convicted."

He glanced at me as he came to a stop at an intersection. The sound of his blinker seemed loud in the near-total quiet. "A first-hand account goes a lot further than just hearsay. They'll want to hear what happened in your own words with all the details. Then they'll be able to find her guilty and give her a proper sentence."

He made it sound so cut and dry. Nothing like I was imagining with drama and lots of yelled objections. "I can't thank you enough for bringing me. It's been a huge relief knowing that I had your support from the beginning on this."

"It's absolutely not a problem," Don said, reaching a hand up to rub the back of his neck. "I'm just happy that I could be here when you needed me."

He pulled into the courthouse parking lot, and nerves made me fall silent again, my brief respite from stress disappearing.

I let myself out. When Don came around to walk with me, his hand went toward the middle of my back to steer me in the right direction. At his touch, my thoughts went to Wes. My nerves flared, and I couldn't help but wonder if I should have brought Wes with me instead. I liked Don. He was very nice, handsome, and had been a huge support through this ordeal. Yet my mind kept drifting back to Wes, my British vet.

Don kept us moving toward the courtroom, staying on the right side of me. Maggie appeared on my left.

"Thank you," I mouthed to her with a smile, turning my head so Don couldn't see me talking to thin air. Maggie nodded and kept up as we headed to the correct courtroom.

I filled my lungs with a deep breath to steady myself.

"It's going to be okay," Don said as he gave me a reassuring smile. "We'll get you through this safe and sound. You'll see. You won't even have to yell something like 'You can't handle the truth.'"

A tight smile crossed my lips.

We passed easily through security and down silent halls to a large wooden door. A tall man in a police uniform opened the door to reveal another door. Making our way through the second door, we found ourselves in a mostly empty courtroom. Just a handful of people observed from the crowd, situated on long benches. Several of them looked to be there on other business. But of the few people there, I did recognize the local shop owners, my friends, all sitting together.

A lump lodged in my throat, and I had to steady myself on the closest railing before I could let Don show me to a seat near the front. It was incredibly kind that they'd all come to support me. The knot of nerves lessened just a little, and a smile brightened my face as I took a seat.

The side door opened and with it, a chill swept across me. I'd started to think I was going to be okay when the bailiff brought Kim into the courtroom.

My body responded to her presence in the same room as mine. Each of my breaths became labored, and I couldn't get warm. I rubbed my hands together, trying to be inconspicuous, and I bit down to keep my teeth from chattering.

Was this a psychological or paranormal response?

Don slid an arm around my shoulders as we all were instructed to rise as the judge entered the room.

The courtroom proceedings began, but I zoned out. Everything ran through my head as I tried to keep it all straight. Stressed out, I couldn't concentrate on anything the court officials were saying.

"Margaret McAllister, please approach." *Oh, double Scotch Bonnet. That's me.*

Don stood when I did. "Good luck," he whispered in my ear, the words of encouragement giving me a slight boost of courage. "I'll be here when it's over."

I glanced at Kim as I made my way to the stand. She studied her hands in her lap. Her face was so forlorn, and she seemed sad. Every part of her drooped. Did she feel remorse?

Well, good. I hoped she did. As though she felt my eyes on her, she brought her chin up. Not able to look at her any longer, I avoided meeting her gaze. *I* couldn't afford to feel guilty for having her prosecuted. She needed to be held responsible for her actions.

Once on the stand, the bailiff asked me to state my name, raise my right hand, and swear to tell the truth. Then the bailiff told me I could take my seat, and an attorney approached.

"Can you state your name again for the record?"

I gulped and shifted in my seat. "Mags, uh, Margaret McAllister."

"Margaret," the prosecutor started. "Do you mind if I call you Maggie?"

I nodded. "Er, Mags, actually. Maggie was my ancestor." I couldn't help but glance at her, still seated on the other side of Don, with an empty space saved between them. "I'm Mags."

Maggie smiled encouragingly, and Don did, too.

"Okay, Mags," the prosecutor continued. "I know testifying today can bring up some rather painful memories, so if at any time you need to, we can take a moment, okay?"

I nodded, swallowing hard. "Yes."

"How long have you known Ms. Hough?" the attorney questioned.

"A few years? Um, we met several years ago when she applied to work in our candle shop." I found myself struggling to remember details and not accidentally say the wrong thing.

The ADA, who seemed like a sheep with the eyes of a lion, smiled. "What about her character? Was she kind? Helpful? A hard worker?"

I nodded. More truths. She'd been a stellar assistant. "Yes, she was a wonderful worker. We never had any issues until that last week when it became obvious that she was trying to sabotage us from delivering some historical documents to a museum." I twisted the button at the bottom of my shirt to help keep me focused. "There weren't any signs that she intended to hurt us until she started the fires."

"So walk me through this timeline," the ADA said, pulling out a copy of Don's report.

For the next few minutes, he asked me about every point in the file. Kim following me, the fires, the documents. Everything.

"How were you able to put the pieces together, Mags?" he asked after finishing Don's report.

"There was a fire in the shop, and we couldn't figure out why someone would want to do that to our business. Then there were several attempts to break into my home, which caused me to go stay with my aunt."

I basically recounted what the attorney had just read from the report, but emotion filled my voice. I fought to keep tears from my eyes. Deep breaths helped me focus, and I tried not to look at Kim as I explained how I'd found the papers in the attic. "The only person I'd told was Aunt Linda, and she'd been at the shop. Kim was the only one in the store at the time. Thankfully, I'd put the papers in my bag when I raced out. Otherwise, I would have been in the house when it caught on fire." I shuddered at the memory.

Kim would've happily and easily killed me for those stupid papers that hadn't had much of an impact on anything. There'd been no big news articles, no explosive confessions in the tabloids. Nobody cared that some random Revolutionary War general, mentioned in the papers, had been a bad man.

I took a shaky breath and gripped the railing in front of me. My gaze strayed to the burn on my arm. I lifted my chin, my heart still thumping heavily in my chest. "When I confronted Kim with my suspicions, she confessed to being behind the whole thing—the fires, everything. It had all been to give her a chance to find the papers and destroy them before we could make them public."

The ADA steepled his hands and bowed his head. "Thank you, Mags, for your willing testimony. If the defense has no further questions, then I ask that the witness be dismissed." The ADA turned to give them a chance to protest. My glance strayed to the person I had been trying to avoid.

Kim mouthed, “I’m sorry.”

Remorse, regret, and guilt… All the things I wanted her to feel seemed to play across her face. It startled me, and I didn’t know what to do.

“Actually,” the defense attorney said, standing from his seat. “I’d like to cross-examine.”

The judge nodded his assent, and my blood ran cold. In all the talks we’d had, the prosecutor had made it seem like they wouldn’t want to risk asking more questions.

“According to your testimony, you said that Kim was an ideal employee, correct?” He practically oozed snake venom.

“Y-Yes,” I said. “But—”

“And when Chief Oswald interviewed you about the fire in your store, do you remember what you told him?”

“I mentioned that I’d done a candle

making demonstration for some customers before, but—"

"And did you tell the Chief that you couldn't remember the condition of your candles at the time of the fire?"

"Well, I—"

"In fact, according to Chief Oswald's report, you said… And I quote, 'I have been a little in my head today.'"

"Yes, but—"

"And did you see Kim, your admittedly excellent worker, set the fire or act in a way that was negligent in the handling of hazardous materials when the fire started?"

"No, Kim was working then."

"Thank you, Miss McAllister. No further questions, Your Honor."

My mouth opened and closed a few times like a fish struggling to breathe out of water. I felt dizzy like I was falling. Maybe I did need one of those air sickness bags Dom had suggested.

"You may step down, Miss McAllister," the judge ordered. It all sounded so official. So much for testifying being boring and not like the movies where actors screamed at one another about not being able to handle the truth.

My temper began to rise, and I could practically feel the steam coming out of my ears. Kim had just apologized to me. Why? Because apparently, her defense was going to be to try to pin everything on me. Double-double Scotch Bonnet. I clamped my lips closed, crossed my arms, and tried to keep my ire off my face. When I glanced at Don for reassurance, he stood and placed a hand on my shoulder, guiding me out of the courtroom.

“It’s a foolish gambit for her attorney to take. There’s plenty of factual evidence tying Kim to her crimes,” he whispered to me. “You’re not going crazy. I promise. Give it time and the ADA will make sure she pays for her crimes.”

Anger poured off me in waves, and I wasn’t sure I could calm down. How dare she nearly murder my aunt, burn down our property, and then try to drag me under the bus.

“I’m testifying after lunch,” Don said as I propped myself against a wall. “I’ll set the record straight about what happened and how Kim was involved.”

CHAPTER SIX

Don glanced at his watch to ensure that he had enough time to make it back before recess was over. "Would you like for me to drive you home?"

I considered bailing on the proceedings. But, no, angry or not, I'd be on tenterhooks waiting to see the outcome. "No, thank you. I need to stay and see this through."

Besides, I wanted to see Don's testimony and Aunt Linda's testimony.

"In that case…" He held out an arm. "Shall we take a walk and get some fresh air?"

"Yes, please." I slid my hand into the

crook of his arm. Getting away from the pressure of the courtroom was a great idea.

"This way," he said, leading me toward the exit.

The other shop owners stood just outside the courthouse doors, waiting for me. Each of them had a mixture of outrage and sympathy on their faces.

Don released me, and I moved forward as they surrounded me in hugs. Each one held me for a moment and whispered something encouraging to me. It did a lot to bolster my mood, knowing I had such a great support system in town. They'd all arranged to leave their businesses, getting employees to cover them during the middle of the day. It meant more than they could know.

As I clung to them, I noticed Maggie. She stood next to Don with sad eyes. Even my ancestor was trying to show her support. If Linda could've been here, we would've been clinging and hugging, too.

Tears welled up when I considered my friends.

"We have to get back to work." Lacy squeezed my hand. "Let us know how things turn out."

Each one smiled and offered more words of encouragement as they left. Don returned to stand next to me as I waved to my friends.

"I know I've said it before but thank you. This day wouldn't have been bearable if you hadn't been here for me."

"Ready for our stroll?" he asked.

I placed my hand on his arm again, and we made our way down the stairs for some fresh air. Quiet with our thoughts, we walked for a while in companionable silence.

Don broke the silence. "You did a great job up there. You were confident and sure of what you were saying." His words warmed me. "You told the truth, and it showed that you cared for Kim." He squeezed my arm. "The jury is smart. They'll see through the lies to the evidence. And I'm sure they'll consider that the defense just tried to revictimize you."

I nodded, not sure what to say. I'd felt like a half-blubbering mess up there. I couldn't even recall most of what I'd said.

"How about a change of subject?" Don suggested.

"That would be nice," I agreed.

When Don cleared his throat, I turned to him. His cheeks seemed redder than they'd been before.

"Are you going to the upcoming town hall ball?" he blurted.

I smoothed my hand over my forehead. "With everything else going on, I'd completely forgotten. As much as I'd like to go, I don't have any plans to."

He beamed. "This year, the historical society—and everyone else, for that matter, too—is wearing Victorian-era outfits for the theme." A big grin spread across his face. "It's supposed to be bigger than normal."

Oh, Victorian-era costumes would be so much fun. "That's awesome. I'll have to reach out to the historical society and see if they want to use any of our hand-dipped candles for the table centerpieces." I clapped my hands together in excitement as ideas began to fill my mind. "Long tapered candles might work as well." And I could video the process and my getting ready. And maybe do some live at the ball. My followers would eat that up.

Don nodded. "Wonderful idea. I took a few old books to the library from the historical society to help Kira out. I think they'll be using them for decorations on the tables." I couldn't help but smile as his chest puffed slightly, filling his suit jacket a little more. "I just kept putting more books in the car until the squad car was overflowing. Books kept trying to escape."

Laughter spilled from me. It was so easy to be around Don. I could appreciate his sense of humor.

"I'm looking forward to going to the ball. It will be a fun evening. Would you like to go together?" He coughed and cleared his throat. "Uh, with me?"

I took a couple of steps before I realized he'd stopped, and I'd left him behind. Looking back at the off-duty officer in his well-cut suit, I considered his offer. It would be a fun evening with Don, but I'd also enjoyed my date with Wes. I would've enjoyed going to the historical society ball with him, but Wes hadn't been around lately, so maybe he wasn't interested. He'd been gone on family business, though. Perhaps he hadn't *wanted* to be gone. But if that was the case, he could've called and he hadn't.

Don was here, and he'd asked me to go with him. What a conundrum.

It dawned on me that I'd started walking again, and Don was still standing behind me, waiting for my answer. I spun back toward him and clasped my hands in front of me. "Yes, I'd love to go with you to the ball as your date."

He beamed as I rejoined him, and we turned to walk back toward the front of the courthouse.

As we reentered the courthouse, it

was obvious Don was fighting to keep his big grin off his face. He gave up and smiled at me, happy about my answer. It was nice to be wanted.

"We can work out the details later, but I think we have to head back to our seats now." He frowned as he guided me back toward the courtroom. "At least your hard part is over."

Yeah, but waiting could be just as bad. Instead of sitting where we had earlier, he moved toward the other side of the room where his fellow cops were seated. As we settled with his cop buddies around us, he leaned in and whispered, "Since I have to take the stand, I wanted you to have someone to sit with that you'd feel safe with."

The judge re-entered before I could say anything or thank him. Instead of speaking, I squeezed Don's hand in appreciation.

Moments later, we were all seated, and they called Don to the stand. I listened intently as he recounted coming to my house and the evidence they gathered. "Mags and Linda were fearful about what this person stalking them wanted. There was no way they could protect themselves until they uncovered the reason that the person would want to hurt them." He laid it all out factually. Short and without any extras so that it all made complete sense. The jury watched with rapt attention. Though, to be fair, Don was easy to listen to.

When they dismissed Don, he came to sit next to me. I patted his knee in a show of solidarity, and Aunt Linda took the stand. She was slightly emotional, like me, and said pretty much the same things I'd said, and Don had said. What else could she say? We were telling the truth, so all our stories matched.

The day ended without any progress that I could see. But the jury had all the details and information they needed for their deliberation so they could find Kim guilty.

The next day, the defense had witnesses I'd never heard of. They were mostly character witnesses, a psychiatrist, and so on. All of them gave opinions rather than facts. I took it as a good sign, but the hours of the trial dragged on until they all began to blur together. Finally, the judge announced that closing arguments would start the following week.

At his words, relief flooded me. We left with smiles on our faces, hopeful that justice would prevail. Don gave me another ride home as he had yesterday. Our companionable silence had continued through our second day together.

"Has your job been much quieter since I've stopped calling you every day with problems?" I asked, only half-joking. I'd been a lot of drama for him for a while there.

"Oh, much. Why, ma'am, it's downright boring most days." He winked at me, and we both laughed.

"Thanks again for the ride." I smiled and waved as I hopped out. "See you next week."

CHAPTER SEVEN

I trudged into the house, drooping with exhaustion, only to find Maggie waiting for me in the entryway. The somber expression on her face broke my heart. I wished I could offer her comfort somehow, but I couldn't hug her or anything. The only help I could give her was to help her move on.

"The trial is on recess until next week," I said, prepping a kettle. "I'll go tomorrow and see if I can search for something more about you. It's been so busy, and I'm truly sorry that I haven't made more progress."

Maggie nodded with a still-solemn expression before she faded out of sight.

It was late enough in the day that I could justify a shower and PJs before I settled in for an early night. This week had been long, hard, and emotionally draining. The knowledge that Kim's fate would be decided weighed on me. It would be based on all the evidence, the facts we'd presented as we sat there in the courtroom day after day. But we would be directly responsible for her future. No, *she* was responsible. I knew that, but the truth of it hung over me.

The kettle whistled, and I poured steaming water over my tea ball. I took a seat, warming my hands on the mug, finally allowing myself to feel more relaxed after such a long day. Aunt Linda would need an update before my shower. She'd elected to spend the day at the shop, prepping everything for the grand re-opening rather than attend another day of the trial. I dialed her number.

"Hello?" she said almost before the first ring had gone through.

"Hey, Auntie. I should give you an update of how things went today."

"I suppose so," she sighed. "Well, don't keep me in suspense. Out with it."

I chuckled at her lack of enthusiasm. "They're ready for closing arguments next week. Depending on how long the jury is out, we might know the verdict by the end of the week. Waiting on them is going to be the hard part."

"How are you holding up, Mags?"

I grimaced. My aunt always went straight to the heart of the problem. "Not great, for sure, but I'm ready for this to be over so we can move on. Speaking of moving on, are the repairs still on schedule?" I didn't wait for her answer to the first question before moving to the next. "Oh, and is there any way we could make some candles for the historical society for the ball?"

She gasped. "Mags, that's a wonderful idea. It'll be a great way to promote the shop's reopening. The timing is almost perfect." I could hear the smile in her voice.

"I thought so, too. This will be the perfect opportunity to do a few TikTok videos while I get the candles ready for the historical society ball." I was already planning the videos in my head. *New content, yay!* "We don't have a new assistant yet, so it'll all be on us."

"Hmm," Aunt Linda answered. "There's a big order that arrived at the end of business today. It's going to take me most of the day tomorrow to sort through." She tsked. "But we can start working on centerpieces after that."

"Okay, I was going out to the house tomorrow to dig around, but I can push that off for later and come over to help you get this giant order sorted, if you need me. Do you want me to come help?"

"Phooey, I had forgotten that we were going to do that tomorrow. You should still go. We need to get everything we can from the house. The weather isn't going to stay dry forever, and nature has a way of taking things over. When this order is finished, I'll join you over there."

Her tone changed to one of excitement. "What if you did one of those video things about the house?"

"Um, well, it's the same kind of content that I normally provide, but I could do a live video." I paused. "In fact, I think that'll make a great one." I didn't want to rain on her idea parade, since I'd already planned on doing one. "It can't hurt to try. It might even be a lot of fun." It would *definitely* be a lot of fun. "I'll think about it and get there a little earlier than you will. It won't hurt to sort things until you get there."

"Sounds like a plan, dear. Get some rest. I'll be home in a little while." Aunt Linda hung up.

I slumped back, mug resting gingerly between my hands as Shadow curled up on my lap. Feeling her little warm body on my legs and the rhythmic purring put all thoughts of a hot shower out of my mind. Maybe I could just sit here for a moment or two.

Blinking as the sun broke through the window, I reached down to pet Shadow only to find she'd abandoned me sometime during the night. I'd gotten used to her coming or going whenever it suited her fancy, but I preferred to wake up to her cute, furry face. Throughout my entire breakfast, I worked on the best way to answer questions from viewers on old posts. And tried to stretch away the discomfort from falling asleep on the couch.

By the time I'd managed to do a couple of response videos, it was almost time for an early lunch. I needed to take a break from TikTok anyway, and Otto's sounded beyond amazing at this point. I parked in the small parking lot and hurried to beat the rush.

"Mags! How are you?" Otto exclaimed in greeting me when I stepped inside. "Any word from the lawyers?"

I shook my head in frustration. "Not yet. I'm all right. It's been hard, but I'm doing better than I thought I would be."

He placed food on a plate, knowing

what my order would be without me having to place it, and handed it to me. "Enjoy."

I sniffed the club sandwich. It smelled as delicious as it always did. So did the chips Otto sliced and fried on-site. "It's terrible that Kim turned out that way. What's even worse is that we have to find someone to replace her. I'm not happy about it, but I know we need the help."

"That is completely understandable. You can't just throw all those feelings away as if they never happened."

I took a bite and moaned with pleasure. Then I held up the sandwich. "So good, Otto. As always."

He grinned. "Just for you, Mags. Just for you." Then he grunted before he went back to helping the other customers while I finished my lunch. After, I decided to stop at the shop to check on Aunt Linda before heading out to the house.

Aunt Linda was in the back, away from most of the renovation noises. Only one contractor was working, but there didn't seem to be much happening.

"Looks like a slow day in here," I called as I stepped over a pile of supplies to reach the back room.

Aunt Linda popped up from behind a stack of boxes. "There you are, darling."

"Where do you want me to start working?" I picked up a couple boxes of new scents and checked them over.

"No, I'll finish this up," she said, taking the boxes out of my hands. "I've just about got the last of it taken care of. Go ahead, head out to the house. I won't be far behind you."

"Only if you're sure." I felt guilty leaving all the work for her to take care of while I went off to dig through an attic and make videos.

"Yes, now, shoo. You're distracting me from getting it all done." She pointed at the exit. "Now go. Love you."

"All right. I'm going, then," I called, making my way back to the front of the shop where I'd parked.

She disappeared behind the boxes again.

Time to explore the attic. I couldn't help but be excited to rummage through old stuff. What would we find? There had to be something to do with Maggie up there, and if I could find it, maybe I could help free her from being stuck in the mortal realm.

There had to be a reason Maggie had protected the attic from burning up in the fire.

CHAPTER EIGHT

As I left the shop, I spotted Shadow waiting for me near my car. She hopped up onto my hood and meowed at me, so I scooped her up and put her in the car. She settled down on the passenger seat. She could've made her way on her own, but I liked her company. Besides, she could explore at Aunt Linda's with me.

The drive out to Aunt Linda's house was uneventful. Though, my jaw slacked when I saw the newly reinforced areas in the middle of the burned areas. The whole thing looked more like a quilt than a house at this point with beams installed from the ground all the way to the ceiling for support to the attic. They'd stabilized the upper level so we could retrieve as much as possible.

Now was the perfect moment to start my live video.

After I let Shadow out of the car, I grabbed my cell and pressed start. After waiting a few minutes for people to start joining the livestream, I flipped the camera around to my face and started my intro. "Welcome back, my Wax Wonders! I told you about the fire at the shop. But what I didn't mention is that my aunt's home was also set on fire. I still can't talk about the particulars while the trial is still ongoing, but most of her house went up in flames. The one saving grace was that, remarkably, the attic appears to be untouched.

"But, if you've ever built a house of cards before, you know how dangerous it can be to have all that area unsupported, so for a while now, they've been stabilizing the house. Today, I'm about to go through things and see what treasures can be discovered up there. For the first time," I added dramatically.

More people began finding the stream, and I had over a hundred watchers in just the first few minutes. As I tiptoed through the wreckage of the living room, I considered how much to tell them. I had some obligation to protect the ongoing prosecution. Until Kim was declared whatever she was going to be declared and the verdict was official, I had to be careful.

Plus, I didn't want to bring Kim into it because that would give her attention. She didn't deserve any attention, especially not after trying to accuse me of being a liar.

Instead, I flipped the camera and panned around the burned remains. "Today is the first day it's been safe for us to come back into the house. I'm really looking forward to seeing what was up there."

With care, I began to ascend the stairs. The chat whizzed by quickly as comments and questions poured in. I still wasn't certain the stairs were as safe as the structural company had claimed. But one hesitant, scary step at a time, I made my way up to the attic.

"Did one of your candles catch the house on fire?" Of course, that would be the first question.

"No, it wasn't a candle. Someone intentionally set the house on fire in the same way they did the shop. Allegedly," I added quickly. I was really beginning to hate that stupid word. We knew Kim had caused the fires, but until she was found guilty, I had to tiptoe around things.

The questions kept coming, rapid-fire. Even in slow mode, there were simply too many questions to keep up with.

Another viewer asked, "What do you plan to do with the house?"

"It's my aunt's home, so it'll be her decision. If I get a vote, I'd like to see her restore it. It's been in the family for many generations, and I grew up here."

With shaky legs, I finally arrived at the second floor. It looked rough.

Deciding to skip the ruined floor, I gave it a quick pan with the camera but didn't set foot on the landing. Instead, I continued up the next flight of stairs. When I reached the top, I scanned the area with the phone to give everyone a view of the clean, functional space that I'd never had a chance to dig through before.

Incredibly, all the boxes were neatly labeled. Everything was organized for us to find things without searching through everything. Well, I'd had plenty of chances but never any inclination before now.

"Should I open the box labeled family heirlooms?" I pointed the camera to another box. "Or the one labeled *legal documents*?"

The resounding answer was the legal documents.

I chuckled and nodded. "You got it." I pulled the box out of the stack and leaned my camera phone on another stack of boxes. From there, my viewing audience could see what I found while not being able to read the words on the papers in case there was something super sensitive… like an address or something else reasonably private.

"Let's see." I pulled a huge stack of papers out of the box. "Wow. There's a lot here."

I started rifling through the pile. "Here's the deed for the house." It was old and interesting, but nothing on it they couldn't see, so I held it up and focused the camera. "Pretty cool. Especially with the old-fashioned seal here." Setting it aside, I looked through the next several pages. "Some stuff that goes with the family's shop, kind of boring." I set those aside and paused, staring down at the next two papers.

"My parents' death certificates," I remarked quietly. "Even with as long as they've been gone, it's still hard to look at this." I didn't want to start crying on a live video, so I set the certificates aside to go over later, privately. After clearing my throat, I glanced at the next page and brightened. "Oh, nice. Easily the most interesting one so far. It's a blueprint of the house."

I held it up so the viewers could see it. "It shows two stories, plus the attic, but this house doesn't have a basement." Setting the phone against a box so I could look closer, I spoke the question I was thinking out loud. "Why would it have a basement listed?"

Another question popped up, drawing my attention. I read it aloud for the viewers. "What if it isn't a basement? Instead, what if it could be tunnels underneath the house?"

I stared at myself in the phone and shrugged. "Could be." Squinting, I held the paper closer to my face, trying to decipher the complicated plans. "Oh, look." I angled it so they could, hopefully, see as well. "It says the entrance is in the pantry, behind the shelves."

Furrowing my brow, I looked directly at the camera. I pointed at the spot that specified the entrance. "Now that can't be labeled correctly. No one has ever mentioned tunnels or anything else below this house. Ever. There's a pantry, but there wasn't another doorway in that room."

With a shrug, I set the blueprints aside and began to search through some of the other documents. "Maybe there's something else here that will explain the discrepancies in the blueprints."

After a few moments of not finding anything of interest in the box, I checked the comments.

"Go see if the door is still there," *CassieOwensGirlMom* urged.

"We need to know if there are tunnels," *Huggyjo* pleaded.

"We're dying here!" *KaraLoki93* was obviously invested.

When there were over forty comments, I finally gave in to their pleas to explore.

"Okay, okay. Let's go exploring to see if that door is actually there." Laughing, blueprints in hand, I descended the stairs slowly.

Not only because I was still a bit worried about the rickety-factor but going too fast would have been nausea-inducing on the video. When we reached the lowest level of the house—floor level, I hurried toward the pantry. Once there, I moved the camera so viewers could see the burned-out pantry was a large room with no other entrances leading out of it.

"See? There's no tunnel entrance." I turned the camera to my face and shrugged wryly at them.

"Break down the wall," Cassie-OwensGirlMom suggested.

Oh, no. Bad idea. "Break it down? We're already sitting here in a burned-out husk of a structure, and you want me breaking walls? No thank you. I'm not really the adventurous type. I'm not Indiana Jones or Lara Croft. I won't find any treasure by breaking walls apart." I laughed at the idea because it was so far out of my comfort zone. "I don't think so."

Huggyjo commented again. "Maybe you could knock on them to see if they sound hollow. Do all the walls sound like the other walls?"

"I like how you think, Huggyjo." It couldn't hurt to knock.

I tried the first wall and then moved on to the others. I returned to the first wall, and my test knock gave off a different sound than the other walls. I tried again, quickly going from one wall to another. Sure enough, one of them sounded hollow.

"You guys…" I propped the phone up on one of the blackened shelves of the pantry and pulled out the blueprints. "They show a closet next to the pantry."

Looking back at the phone, I nodded at the suggestion that I push on the walls. It didn't take much to move the obstruction. With a slight shove, the wall gave slightly. As I used more force, it moved even more.

"Oh, my gosh, y'all!" I exclaimed. "Are you guys seeing this?"

The corner where the walls should have met was a cracked seam, but the other corners of the room were smooth. *Oh, man. Oh, man.* My mouth dried, and I studied the ceiling, hoping what was left of it wouldn't come crashing down on me. I was about to knock down a wall in a burned-out house… at the urging of social media. I smoothed my hand over my forehead. Was I really going to knock down the wall? I grinned. *Of course I am.*

My camera needed to be settled in the best spot to show me as I tried to open the fake wall. I fiddled with the camera spot and ignored the increasing number of comments begging me to knock it down already. I had hundreds watching my escapades in real-time. Maybe even close to a thousand by now.

When I was happy with the camera placement, I turned to the wall. I rubbed my hands together. Then I used my nails to slide the crack open a little more. When I pried harder, it moved.

Shocked, I turned, but the wall came with me. It was surprisingly light, and I leaned it against one of the sturdy pantry walls. A draft blew up toward me, bringing a musty smell with it.

Behind the wall was an empty space,

leading down. A staircase was there as if it was beckoning me to explore.

I gasped and tried to contain my excitement as I read the comments flooding the live stream. I flashed two thumbs up. "Well, looks like the blue-prints were right after all. Good call on knocking, Huggyjo."

I checked the screen. Yep. A few thousand people were now watching, and some of them complained about how dark everything was. That was an easy fix.

"I need another flashlight," I updated everyone as the stairs led into total darkness. "I can't see much of anything."

There should've been a flashlight in the hall closet. It had been there for every power outage there'd ever been through my growing-up years. "Hang on, I'll be right back."

Hurrying out to the hall, I sifted through all the ash and soot before I discovered one at the bottom. It was in pretty good shape, despite being surrounded by burned house. It was a little ironic I had to dig for what I needed to find more clues.

I wanted to rush back, but I needed to catch my breath and keep calm. Plus, the open passageway would build suspense and get more people into the live. This was going to be huge, regardless of what I found. I walked quickly back to the pantry, grabbed the phone, and turned it around toward my face, grinning at the thousands of people waiting to see what happened. "Okay, here we go. Y'all better have my back if this goes sideways."

I turned on the flashlight and pointed the camera down, descending slowly into the cool underground stairwell. "Isn't this amazing?" I crooned, and my voice echoed up and down the narrow tunnel.

At the end of the stairs was another door. "Okay. We've got another door."

A question from *ReptileWoman* popped up asking if I really didn't know about any of this hidden stuff or if I was faking it.

"I swear, I had no idea any of this existed. This isn't some stunt. I'm as stunned as you guys are. Hold on while I try to open this so we can keep going."

I sat the phone and flashlight on the stairs behind me, so it could keep filming as I tried to open the next door. Both hands went around the knob as I placed a foot at the base of the door frame.

After a few good tugs, I jerked backward, and the door came free from the frame. The momentum sent me flying back, and I landed smack on my rear. When I looked up, a man dressed in Victorian attire stood there on the other side of the doorway, staring at me in shock.

I let out a scream as my flashlight died, the phone fell over, and everything plunged into darkness.

CHAPTER NINE

The echo of my scream reverberated in the sudden darkness. My heartbeat thundered in my ears, and I could feel my veins pulsing in my fight or flight terror.

With my eyes finally starting to adjust to the dark, I scanned the space for my phone; after all, there should be some sort of light coming from it or something. The harder I looked, the more frantic I became. I needed to be able to get back up the stairs without dying, and if I couldn't find my phone, I'd have to find the flashlight and pray it would work.

"I'm okay," I whispered to myself. Even as a grown adult, it was hard not to be afraid of the dark when the dark was in a creepy secret tunnel under a burned-out house. I took a deep breath of air and slowly released it, trying to slow the pounding of my heart. I smoothed my hand over the ground until my hand closed around my phone.

Louder, I repeated, "I'm okay! The flashlight died as I opened the door, and I landed on my rear. I'll have to go back upstairs and calm my nerves for a bit. Maybe get a more reliable flashlight. Don't worry, I'll update you all later. Probably on YouTube, rather than trying to go live again. Nobody call the cops. I am okay, and it's still just me. Stay tuned for the next update, stay safe and burn bright."

With that, I ended the live stream. How was that for a cliffhanger? I collapsed on the ground and shook my head. I took another deep breath. That was a mistake, because it was filled with dirt and dust from the door being opened so abruptly.

I turned on the phone's flashlight, and its paltry light flooded the darkness with enough light…for now.

Where did the man in the doorway go?

A pitter-patter sounded on the stairs, and I glanced up to see Shadow coming down the steps toward me. I climbed to my feet. "Fancy meeting you here. Do you know the guy in the suit?"

She meowed at me and then didn't hesitate to enter the dark tunnel leading into the unknown, so I followed her. Why not? The corridor emptied into a large room. Or what seemed to be a large room, the best I could tell with my phone flashlight.

In the first corner, a rock alcove had been built into the wall.

Shadow jaunted around the room as though she still had no fear of this place or what might lurk around the corner. I spun slowly, trying to hit as much of the space with my light as possible.

That was when I saw *him. Again.* He was on the opposite side of the room from the alcove.

"Hello there. I didn't mean to scare you," the man said, giving a slight bow from the waist. "I'm Viscount William Howe the Seventh."

The Seventh… Had he said the Seventh? My breath came in short bursts as questions flew through my mind. My thoughts spun.

"How long have you been down here?" I finally blurted out.

He pursed his lips and clasped his hands behind his back. "The year eighteen seventy, I believe. That was the year I came to the Americas from England." He gave a weary sigh. "It has been so very long since I have spoken to anyone."

"Why are you still down here?" I tried not to squeal, but I'm pretty sure I did. Gesturing around me, I tried to take surreptitious glances around. "Why are you still down here?" I repeated in a whisper this time.

He shrugged elegantly. “I didn’t fulfill my purpose.”

Aunt Linda’s voice echoed faintly from somewhere above me. I smiled tentatively at the…Viscount? “Listen, I’ve got to go find my aunt. She’s upstairs. Can you, I mean, are you able to come *with* me?” I hated to leave him down here alone after he’d just found me.

“I will wait for you to return.” He nodded stiffly. “I’m unable to leave this portion of the dwelling. My body is buried here, and I’m connected to it.”

Aunt Linda called for me again. “Mags?”

I had to run, so I raised a finger. “Wait here. I’ll be right back. I promise.”

“I hadn’t planned to go anywhere,” he answered with a frown.

Thankfully, the light increased as I made my way up the disused stairs and found Aunt Linda at the base of the attic.

“Where on earth were you, Mags?” She sounded exasperated and her face matched her voice. She frowned at me. "You're filthy. Have you been rolling in… dust… and, and cobwebs? And I thought you were checking the attic?" She plucked a cobweb from my hair and tried to toss it aside, but it stuck to her until she wiped it on her pant leg.

Without answering her question, I asked one of my own. "I found blue-prints for the house up there. Did you know about the tunnels under the house?"

Her bracelets rattled as she waved her hand and laughed. "It sounds like something out of your mystery novels."

I ignored her dismissal. "Exactly what I thought until I *found* the tunnel listed on the blueprint." I grabbed her hand and dragged her to the pantry.

At the pantry, her mouth fell open when she saw the removed wall with a stairway leading down. "You weren't joking."

"No. Definitely not joking." I bounced in place. "I was doing a live stream and inspecting the walls. This one moved. I pulled it out and found the staircase."

The phone's flashlight turned on with the flick of my finger.

"That's not all I found. There's a…" Before the rest of the sentence could leave my lips, Viscount William stood in the doorway looking at us.

"Aunt Linda, may I present Viscount William Howe the Seventh." I hoped I remembered that correctly. "William, this is my Aunt Linda McAllister."

He nodded formally. "Please to meet you."

"Why are you hanging around down there?" Aunt Linda questioned.

I hurried to explain. "He was telling me that his body is down there. He's not allowed to leave it."

William rushed forward, causing Linda to stiffen. Though, she wasn't likely scared at this point. We both had too much experience with ghosts for fright.

"It was many years ago," he explained. "My brother murdered me and left my body in the tunnels to rot." His voice filled with sadness.

The thought of someone being murdered below the house horrified me.

"I am a descendant of General William Howe," he continued. "His journal turned up, and I wanted a chance to dig into his secrets." The ghost ignored the shocked looks on our faces.

"We-we've uncovered a few secrets ourselves," I said in a near-stammer. "In fact, we recently turned all the papers we'd found on General William Howe over to a historical museum to preserve them." The possibility of learning more about what happened during his life was rather exciting.

"Yes, I heard you ladies talking about them, but those were pieces of his professional life," he explained when I gave him a confused look. "The journal is about his personal life and will change the lives of many people. It's filled with violent confessions, and I came here to make things right."

We followed the specter as we

listened in fascination to his story. "My first stop was here, where my brother killed me. I was trying to set things right with Maggie McAllister's family. I know who killed her. It's in the journal. You'll have to dig it up."

He moved toward the corner close to where he appeared earlier and pointed to a pile of rocks. "It's here."

Aunt Linda and I moved the rocks quickly, and within a few minutes, we uncovered the journal. In pristine condition.

I lifted it out of its shallow grave and ran a gentle finger over the cover. "This is so incredible for it to be unharmed."

"I have protected it through the years. As I must now protect someone else." He disappeared.

My curiosity got the better of me as I wandered around looking for any signs of him.

"Do you think he's moved on?" I asked Aunt Linda. "He said he couldn't leave his body, which is presumably here somewhere."

"That's more than likely it. He finished his purpose. Now he can find peace." She nodded at me. "Now let's see what else is down here."

Our phone lights illuminated more tunnels with antiques and other family relics peppered here and there. Candlesticks and antique guns lined the walls.

I looked around in awe. "You're certain that you've never heard of the tunnels before?"

"No." Aunt Linda shook her head. "If I had, then we would have cleared everything out. This isn't my idea of a safe space to store antiques."

I chuckled and studied the historical treasures. What a remarkable find.

CHAPTER TEN

As the new week started, I found myself unable to focus on TikTok videos, candle making, or even the upcoming closing statements at court. The journal called to me, distracting me every moment of every day.

This journal held clues to Maggie's death. Social media would have to wait. Chills ran down my spine as I read through the entries. Several dull stories or self-important bragging filled the pages before I found one entry that turned my stomach.

While on an assignment near Indian Territory, I had to kill my ranking officer. The late

Colonel Jessup. It was really quite unavoidable. The red savages of the land will of course take the blame for his demise.

Further down, another mention of his victim.

They buried Jessup today. It was a lovely service. More than he deserved. As expected, the story about an Indian ambush was sufficient. Scouts even confirmed recent Shawnee raiding parties. My heroics during the encounter have impressed my superiors. There is talk of a promotion.

I bristled at the words and had to place the book aside until I calmed down. The general was a snake.

I turned on my phone and filmed a series of three-minute candle dipping videos for uploading while I calmed down. My meditation as I tried to block out all that—No. Unwilling to get riled up again, I shoved the journal out of my mind.

Later that evening, I tried again to read a little more with Maggie sitting by my side.

We exchanged a glance. Her face was

so hard to read. I hoped she might have some idea if the answers were in the journal.

"Do you think he knew who killed you?" I asked.

All I received in response was a shrug before she disappeared. I harrumphed and set the journal aside again. It might hold answers, but it was hard to read, like trying to sift toxic sludge by hand. I'd try again tomorrow.

Aunt Linda had asked me to stop in the shop the next day to help unpack some supplies. The renovations were almost complete, and it was nice to be back in the shop working again.

She cut open a box and sorted it onto the shelves. "Did you find anything in the journal?"

"He was a horrible man. That's what I found." I shuddered at the things I'd read. "In the journal, he admits to cheating on his wife while he was here in America. Which is certainly bad enough, but he seduced an American soldier's wife to do it."

"Ugh, men like him give all the others a bad name," she spat.

I stopped unpacking to take a call from the historical society, returning my call with color preferences, so I could start working on the candles for their centerpieces.

Aunt Linda smiled as I raced through unpacking the rest of the boxes, in a hurry to get home and get started.

I set everything up and filmed the dipping of the historical society's candles. I'd just set them to music later. The videos of the candles went well, but after a couple of hours, I needed a break.

Drawn to the journal, I *needed* to continue reading it, as much as I hated it. I picked it up again.

The burdens of leadership. I had a young corporal executed for sedition today. Sedition and his unscrupulous tongue when it came to questions about my personal affairs in front of the missus. I forget his name as surely as it will be forgotten by history. At least in death, he sends a bitter reminder to the rest of the men under my command that discretion is the better part of valor.

I could feel my skin crawling. Beyond disgusted once again, I went back to making the candles. The TikToks were a welcome distraction from how horrible his journal made me feel.

I dove in again the next day while waiting for the attendant at the dress shop, with Maggie nearby, wearing as close to a smile as I'd ever seen on her. It was time to find a dress for the ball for my date with Don.

Cecilia is with child. Her husband, the dullard, has been unable to provide for her in such a way. Now she believes it is providence's blessing that she should carry a child now. Of course, the child's true nature must be concealed.

I set the journal aside as the shop attendant arrived with a few Victorian-era pieces. In this old shop, I felt like my ancestor herself, out for a new frock. Who could the child have been when it had grown up?

Maggie nodded at the dress. I'd tried on several, but none of them had seemed to be the right thing. With her help, I felt confident that I would look perfect for this special event.

Purchase complete, I headed home to continue reading. As much as it curdled my stomach, I had to carry on. The man was a *horrible* person. I couldn't imagine anyone staying around him long enough to fall in love with him or carry his child. My mind churned through the journal entries I'd read so far.

Once home, I put my plans to read and make videos on hold when Don called as I was hanging my new dress on a hook in my closet.

"We just got word," he said. "The jury's reached a decision. Would you like to come to the courthouse with me?"

"I'm not sure that I should." I was hesitant to go back. Or anywhere near Kim, for that matter. What if the verdict wasn't what I liked? Would I launch myself across the courtroom at her and get thrown in jail myself?

"No problem. You don't have to,"

Don said. "I can always come by afterward to tell you what the verdict is."

"I think I'd rather that," I admitted rather sheepishly.

"I'll see you in a little while."

"Thank you," I said. "That would be really nice of you."

I set myself to work while I waited, trying to pass the time as quickly as I could, but my plans to work on the videos I needed for upload didn't go so well.

With a huff, I gave up and called Aunt Linda to help keep me from worrying. "Want me to come in and help you get ready?"

"Nah, I think we're good for now. Stay home and relax while you can," she suggested.

Frustrated, I wasn't sure what to do with myself while I waited. I puttered around the house, wiping counters, folding towels. Stuff that could've waited.

Eventually, Maggie appeared beside me. She pointed toward the journal.

Oh, that darn thing. My shoulders

slumped. I was pages and pages into it and nothing good had come up. Mostly, it made me mad a leader could be allowed to be such an awful person. I was already stressed out without reading about how General Howe had been a rotten person.

"Do you really think that's a good idea?"

She shook her head no but still pointed toward it, her face still solemn.

"All right," I agreed, picking it up and finding where I'd left off. I plopped down on the sofa.

A colonial spy has reached out to me, looking for information. There is little risk of these upstarts doing any damage to the British Empire, so what better way to profit from their ill-fated rebellion?

Was he talking about my ancestor? Maggie's brother? I read on.

One of the previous soldiers I trusted is about to sell me out.

Now surely that was Nathan Hale.

This soldier has collected evidence to expose me and plans to use this as a tactic to sow chaos.

He continued the story a few pages later.

The ambitious colonial has been dealt with. Alas, where I had thought his secrets would die with him, Cecilia has notified me of the man's sister. It seems this sister might also have access to the evidence against me. I believe a cleansing fire might be to properly sort out this problem.

I gasped and looked up at Maggie.

"General Howe killed you." I finally had a big missing piece of the puzzle.

CHAPTER ELEVEN

A knock on the door startled me out of my horror.

Even with my attention focused on the door, I had enough foresight to put the journal under one of the chair cushions, out of view. With a roiling feeling in my stomach, I walked over and opened the door.

Don stood on my front stoop with a neutral expression. The verdict. Suddenly, all my nerves and emotions rose back to the surface and turned into a boulder in my throat.

I wasn't sure if I was excited that he was there or just worried about Kim's verdict. Part of me didn't even want to see him, so I didn't have to find out. What if it was bad news? I shuddered at the thought of Kim being set free.

His eyes dropped as he took his cap off to hold in his hands.

"Oh, I'm sorry," I stammered. "Would you like to come in?"

Don shuffled his feet on the wooden planks of the porch. "Nah, I'm on duty. There's a mountain of paperwork waiting for me back at the station." He leaned against the doorframe. "I wanted to tell you in person."

My breath caught. "Tell me what?" It felt like the floor wasn't solid anymore. Had Kim been released?

"They found her guilty," he said. Relief washed over me. "Sentencing is set to start next month."

"Guilty," I breathed. It still didn't feel quite real. But that was it. The jury had found Kim guilty.

"And it wasn't just one or two charges," Dom continued. "They found her guilty on every charge. Arson, stalking, aggravated battery, and a few others. It's a slam dunk for the ADA and the--"

I jerked forward awkwardly and wrapped him in a hug. He returned my embrace, but I pulled back a little, shocked that I'd thrown myself at him. He didn't seem to be too upset by my actions.

"Um, thank you, and um, I'm sorry about that," I apologized, smoothing out wrinkles that weren't on the front of my shirt.

"You're welcome. I'm sorry that all of this stuff happened to you in the first place."

With a nod, I thanked him again for his support and his help through it all.

"Yeah, no problem. Look, we should talk about the ball before I have to go." He fiddled with his hat for a moment, but I couldn't concentrate on anything, much less stringing sensible words together.

So I nodded again, and he continued. "The dance starts at seven, but I have to work the parade first. Would it be okay if I pick you up around six forty-five?"

"Um, sure. I'd like that." Another stupid nod was all I could manage. "It's perfect. I can be ready for you."

His radio started squawking. "I'm so sorry. I have to go."

"Goodbye." I gave a little wave.

But he was already turned around, and he took off running to the squad car.

I stood there, unsure of how I felt. Don was practically perfect, but Wes continued to pop into my head at the most awkward times. Like this.

Should I have reached out to Wes? It'd been too long, and I didn't want to look silly if I reached out now. Especially when I had a date with someone else. Ack.

I went back inside to where Maggie still stood in the entryway. "The journal is going to have to wait a bit," I said, grabbing the book from under the cushions and putting it away. "I need a break."

She nodded to me.

The next day Aunt Linda needed me to help decorate and set up the shop. It was a welcome relief from all the discoveries of the past twenty-four hours.

Arriving bright and early, I only detoured for a cup of coffee. "The journal gave up a few more of its secrets," I told Aunt Linda as I shook my head in disbelief. "General Howe killed Maggie. I just can't read any more yet. It's too much."

"There, there." She patted my shoulder in sympathy. "It's completely understandable to shy away from horrible things like that. Everything you've told me sounds terrible. The man wasn't a hero. I might not want to read anything else."

"Can you believe the way history repeated itself?" I swept up another pile of construction dust. "He burned Maggie alive. That is exactly what Kim was trying to do to us, even if that wasn't her original intention."

"So what do we do now? There

won't be a body for Maggie, and she can't just stay a ghost forever. Can she?" Aunt Linda stopped arranging a display to look at me in concern. "She has to go on to the next place, right?"

"She didn't disappear when we found out who killed her. Maybe there is another way to help her move on and find peace." I shrugged, unsure of what that could be.

Around five, all the businesses closed, and everyone poured out into the streets to watch the parade.

I stayed on the sidewalk in front of the shop until most of the parade had passed. It was time for me to sneak away and get ready for the ball. I didn't want Don to have to wait for me to get dressed.

Shadow waited at the front door when I arrived. I leaned down to pet her before going to the shower. It didn't take as long as I'd thought to get ready, and I finished with time to spare before Don arrived.

Butterflies fluttered in my stomach,

and my thoughts turned to Wes. Was he going to be there tonight?

While I waited, the journal beckoned to me. So I pulled it out, starting where I'd left off, and steeled myself for more confessions from the twisted general.

When the Roman General Scipio defeated Carthage, he salted the earth. Following his tremendous example, I have razed the traitor's family tree. Their family home longed for the torch, and I found myself awestruck by the violent beauty of the destruction. Let that serve as warning to those that would dare cross me. My legacy will be planted in the fertile dirt of my enemies' graves.

A familiar rap on the door shook me from the journal's pages. How could one man could be so ruthlessly evil? With shaking hands, I put the journal away.

I opened the door with a flourish and a smile on my face.

"You look absolutely lovely," Don said, holding out his arm to me.

I grinned as I took it. We made a

dashing pair in our historical garb. "Well, hello there. Don't you look all fancy in that getup?"

His personal truck sat idling outside as he guided me around to the passenger door.

"How did the candle-making work out? Did you get them all done?" Ever a gentleman, he opened the door and held out one hand for me to use as I stepped up on the running board and up into the cab.

I waited for Don to get in the driver's seat before answering. "Yes, and I can't wait to see how they've set them up for the ball. Aunt Linda took all the candles over earlier, so I didn't even get to have a sneak peek."

He chuckled and backed out of my driveway. "Each year, they do such an amazing job. The ball never disappoints."

Conversation flowed easily with Don, as usual, and soon we arrived to find the parking lot almost full of vehicles.

"We aren't late, but it seems we're the last to arrive," I said with a chuckle.

"That's okay." He parked the truck at the back of the lot, then he did the gentlemanly thing once more, helping me out and holding out his arm to walk me in.

I hooked my hand in his offered elbow. The ballroom was full, and we stood just inside the main doorway for a moment, looking around at the beauty of the room and costumes.

I spied Aunt Linda across the room, standing with Maggie next to her in her usual ghostly garb.

Questions filled me, and I decided I needed to speak with her privately about why Maggie was here.

"Are you hungry?" Don asked, "Or maybe you'd like to dance first?" He patted his lapel pocket. "I bought two tickets for the buffet if you'd like to eat now."

My stomach rumbled with hunger right on cue. "Food sounds wonderful. I would love to eat, but I need to run to the restroom first though."

"Sure, I'll be here when you get back." He nodded toward two seats that had just opened. "I'll grab those, so we don't lose them."

As I made my way across the room, I got Aunt Linda's attention. "Follow me," I whispered as I passed her.

We both ended up in the restroom, alone for the moment.

I checked all the stalls to be sure that we didn't have any inadvertent eaves-droppers. "Why is Maggie here?" I hissed. "With you?"

"I honestly don't know." She shook her head in bewilderment. "It looked like she was watching the entrance for someone to come into the ballroom."

"Well, then we'll just have to wait and see who she is waiting for." I nodded with determination. She hadn't followed us to the restroom. When we walked out, we found her in the exact spot we'd left her. I joined Don, draping my shawl over the chairs as I did, so we could grab some food.

"When will the store be open again?" Don made an attempt at idle conversation as we waited in the buffet line, but the room was loud with the music and all the conversation. Small talk was nearly impossible.

"The grand re-opening is tomorrow," I almost yelled. "You should come by and see all the stuff we've done. It looks so amazing."

Don's smile dazzled me, but I found myself searching for Maggie again. I felt so guilty for flirting with him when she was upset.

We returned to our, thankfully, still available seats, and set in to eating, which slowed the conversation for a few minutes. The food was fantastic, but I'd lost most of my appetite, worrying about Maggie.

Don must've noticed my distracted state of mind as we finished everything on our plates. Or, rather, as I pushed the food around my disposable dish. I couldn't help but notice him glancing at me repeatedly as I looked around for Maggie.

After pushing his plate away, he smiled at me encouragingly and rather patiently. "Would you like to dance?"

"Yes, please," I said, taking the hand he offered. If I wasn't so worried about Maggie, this would've been a great time, but right now I needed to monitor the door. Who was she here looking for?

Classical arrangements of popular songs made dancing a simple task. I felt lighter, and all my worries fled with each turn and twist to the music. I almost forgot to keep an eye on the door until I saw Wes walk through.

He was dressed up and looking *so* dashing.

And right behind him came the ghost from the tunnel, William, yelling at Wes at the top of his voice. He was throwing his hands around in the air, panicked and shouting as if everyone could see him instead of only me and Linda.

What in the world?

CHAPTER TWELVE

People twirled and dipped around us, but I stopped dancing and took a step back from Don, completely shocked by the spectacle of ghostly William berating physically bodied Wes.

Don tilted his head as he looked at me. "Are you okay?"

I tracked Don with my peripheral vision because my eyes were focused on Wes and William. But still, I nodded. "Yes," I murmured. "I'm fine."

Don followed my gaze, and his expression fell as he spotted Wes.

"I need to speak to him." I looked

back at Don apologetically. "Sorry to interrupt our dance."

"All right." He sighed, and his brow furrowed. "I'll go get a drink."

It was regrettable that I had upset Don, but strange things were afoot. I rushed over to Wes, doing my best not to look like I was hurrying or desperate to see him. When I got close, I slowed down and affected a serene smile toward Wes, who was still being harangued by the ghost, though he didn't seem to notice anything was wrong.

"Hi there." He smiled at me. "I'm happy to see you." He took a moment to take in my costume. "You look amazing."

"You look wonderful, yourself," I replied, taking in a steadying breath. The last thing I need for him to think I was upset. I was, but he didn't need to know. "Where have you been lately?"

"I've been out of town for a while, and when I returned, the clinic was backed up." He brushed a hand through his hair. "I've been meaning to reach out to you, but I've literally been collapsing into bed each night, exhausted from the long days."

"Hello! Why are you ignoring me?" William yelled, waving his ghostly appendages in Wes' face. "Why won't he listen to me?" he said when he noticed me standing there. "He's been ignoring me all day."

Unsure of what to say, I debated answering the ghost. Though, if I did that, Wes would think I was insane.

I opened my mouth, my gaze darting between Wes and William, but a group of people surrounded us, greeting Wes and me and interrupting my plight with pleasantries.

After they walked away, Wes brought his focus back. "You look really lovely."

The smile I'd pasted on softened. I was going to have to tell him about William, who apparently couldn't cross over yet.

That was when I remembered he'd mentioned that he needed to protect someone else.

Could that person be Wes?

"Can we speak outside?" I motioned to the door he'd just walked through.

Suddenly serious, he nodded yes. I followed him through the ballroom door and to the right, then out a giant set of French doors onto a mezzanine.

The balcony area had a few people off to the side, but we had most of it to ourselves. I cleared my throat. "This is going to sound completely crazy, but there is something I need to tell you."

He leaned against the balcony rail and waited for me to continue. Amusement glowed behind his eyes. That would change when he realized just how crazy this was going to sound.

"Remember when I did that research and you mentioned you were related to General Howe?" I took a deep breath to steady my nerves. "Well, I was trying to find out who had killed my ancestor, Maggie McAllister. It's a long story, with a strange set of events, but ultimately…"

"Ultimately," he echoed, drawing out the word.

"I have a ghost that's haunting me," I said, squeezing my eyes shut so I couldn't see his reaction.

It felt like hours of silence passed. I carefully opened my eyes. Wes burst out laughing, throwing his head back in delight. I raised my eyebrows and waited for him to realize I was serious.

It took several chuckles and a guffaw or two before his laughter started to falter. Another giggle later, he clamped his lips together and blinked rapidly at me. "*What?*"

"Well," I said, struggling to get the rest out. In for a penny, I guess. "Maggie was the first, and now I've found a ghost that is trying to right the wrongs that General Howe committed." This was the part that was going to be the *most* unbelievable for him. "Well, I'm… He's kind of haunting you, right now, but…um, you haven't noticed him."

"That would explain some things," he said after a moment, tipping his head to the side. "I've felt like someone was watching me lately."

Then he'd noticed, without knowing *what* he was noticing. "It's been just this week," he continued. "Odd things here and there. Like doors closing or things being moved around without me having done it. It was starting to freak me out."

William nodded with enthusiasm; his frantic movements forgotten as he listened to Wes. "Yes! I've been trying to get his attention by any means available to me."

I turned to William and spoke to the thin air. At least that was likely how it looked to Wes. "I thought you'd crossed over. What happened to not being able to leave your buried body?"

"I didn't know I could. I sensed danger, then suddenly I was next to Wes. I can go back and forth between him and my body. Nothing else has let me appear near it yet."

There was no way I could stay on the balcony much longer. I glanced at my watch. It'd been five minutes. Don would start looking for me soon.

Wes eyed me curiously.

I motioned toward the ghost, not that Wes could see him. "Yes, William is here." I listened to the ghost explain how he was related to Wes. "And he has some things he wants to tell you."

Wes's eyebrows hit his hairline, but he remained quiet.

I relayed what William said. "When your father passes, you'll become the next viscount."

Wes appeared uncomfortable when I mentioned it. "Yes," he muttered. "It's true."

"William isn't here to hurt you. In fact, he says it's just the opposite." I tilted my head for the next bit of information. "He's here to protect you."

Wes crossed his arms and frowned, but he didn't speak.

"He says that he's not sure why he's drawn to you, but that you are in some sort of danger. You need protection because something bad is coming, and he doesn't want you hurt." I glanced around and discovered Maggie stood just behind me. "Is that why you've appeared as well?"

She smiled serenely.

I nodded in acknowledgment of the warning. "The ghost haunting me is here, too. They came here to warn us of the danger. It's why they're drawn to us."

With another glance at my watch, I tutted my tongue. It'd been eight minutes. This was taking too long.

"Is this why you haven't moved on after I found out who killed you?" I asked Maggie.

Her see-through hair waved as she nodded.

"Who else are you talking to? I mean, who is haunting you?" Wes looked around nervously.

"The ghost of my ancestor is here. Maggie McAlister. She's here to protect me. While William here is trying to protect you."

William shifted from foot to foot, nervous and jumpy. "He needs to read the journal of General Howe, so you can set things straight. Fix the wrongs done by the Howe family."

I relayed the information to Wes. "This isn't happy reading. It's not for the faint-hearted either." I shuddered. "I've been trying to get through it, but I've had to do it in bits."

"Can I come by after the dance to pick it up?" Wes asked.

I gave him a wry smile. "General Howe did some really terrible things. I just want you to be prepared before you dive in. William died trying to right those wrongs. His own brother killed him to keep the journal's secrets from coming to life." I condensed all the information as quickly as I could in the short story version to Wes.

Ten minutes had now passed, as I looked at my watch again, and Wes stood there, staring at me.

I laid a hand on his arm in sympathy. "Are you all right?"

"Yeah, I'm just coming to terms with everything you've told me. There are ghosts. Also history is trying to hurt us.

It's a lot to process." He shook his head in disbelief.

My chuckle cut through the sounds coming from inside. "I understand. I had a hard time in the beginning too. Maggie freaked me out when she first appeared to me. I'll have to tell you about it sometime."

With another look at my watch, I knew it was time to go. "Don is going to come looking for me, so I need to get back inside. But if you want to come by after the dance is over, then you are more than welcome to come and see the journal."

Wes swallowed hard but nodded yes.

I didn't want to be rude to Don, but darn if I wanted to stay out here with Wes and the ghosts. "Bye, William. I'll see you around."

I left Wes on the balcony and hurried back inside.

Don was watching the doorway for me but was talking to some fellow officers. When he saw me, he excused himself and made his way toward me.

"Is everything okay?" he asked with concern.

"Yes," I smiled at him, "for now. Ready for another dance?"

It wasn't fair to Don for my mood to ruin what had been a wonderful evening. So I determined the rest of the night would be amazing.

CHAPTER THIRTEEN

Don dropped me off without a prolonged goodnight. I thanked him for a lovely evening, but even as hard as I tried, we never found that light-hearted flirtation again. Maybe because I wasn't feeling terribly lighthearted.

My hair was curled and full of hair spray. There was no way I'd be able to sleep with all this goop in my hair. The only way to fix the problem was a shower, but I didn't want to miss Wes if he came by.

I turned my cell on high and hopped in the shower, lathering and rinsing as quickly as I could. I didn't hear the doorbell, and my phone didn't make a peep.

Hair clean and brushed to air dry, I worried about Wes as I finished dressing. I hadn't seen him return to the party after I dropped a big family history bomb in his lap. I hoped he was okay.

Shadow was curled up on my bed waiting for me with Maggie by her side.

"Is Wes all right?" I asked her.

She nodded but tilted her head as if she heard something outside of the bedroom.

Cautiously, I left the room, slightly freaked out, as the doorbell rang. I couldn't help feeling nervous. We were dealing with ghosts who wanted to protect us.

But protect us from *what*?

Wes stood there in his period attire when I opened the door. A smile danced across my lips at him in his knickers. "Would you like to come in?" I asked, stepping back to allow him in.

He looked around my living room

like it was his first time seeing it, but of course, it wasn't. He was just on edge. Couldn't blame the poor guy.

Reaching out, I squeezed his wrist gently. "Coffee, or do you drink tea?"

"I could use a cup of tea." His added smile held a hint of desperation.

"Come on." Sadly, I led the way into the kitchen and waved for him to take a seat at the table.

We chatted about nothing serious while we waited for the drinks to be ready. His answers to my questions pretty much stayed short, and while not curt, also were not forthcoming.

Several awkward minutes later, I placed the mug of hot tea in his hand. "The journal is in the other room. I'll go get it for you."

When I returned, he held the mug as if it was the only thing that was real.

I sat the journal between us.

He reached for it, but I placed my hand over his. "Listen. It's a harsh look at his life. He confessed everything he did that was evil. A very detailed look at what a horrible person he was."

With a nod, he took a deep breath. "I'm ready."

"There are details that will make you cringe," I warned and took my hand from his.

With his hand still on the journal, Wes looked at me with his big puppy dog eyes. "I would have told you I was going to become a viscount. Eventually." He pulled the journal toward his spot. "I don't want the title or estate. I've been trying to find a way out of it for years."

After opening the book to the first page, Wes looked back at me. "It's one reason I haven't settled down or tried to start a family. It would lock them into continuing the *lineage*."

Heck. Being a viscount sounded fun to me, but I hadn't grown up with it and whatever all it entailed. "You're just Wes, the vet, to me. My friend. I'm not mad you kept it to yourself. It's hard to explain everything when you first meet someone." I shrugged. "Besides, a title like that might be something a different type of person would go after. You have to be careful until you get to know your friends, I imagine."

He nodded enthusiastically. "That's true. I do. Some people, some women, go after titled men like they're prizes to be awarded."

Looking relieved, Wes sucked in a deep breath and focused on the journal again. "How far did you read in the journal?" He took a sip of his tea.

"I haven't finished it yet, but I got through most of it. Do you want to read it with me here? I can sit with you."

He opened it and read a couple of pages, his eyes widening as they scanned the slanted handwriting. "This is a complete disaster," he declared, slamming the journal shut.

"There are some things that might matter to your family," I admitted with a sigh.

"Like what?" He tilted his head, waiting for me to respond.

"General Howe had a child out-ofwedlock while married to his wife, who remained in England. The baby was with an American soldier's wife."

William appeared at my elbow. "If that story was told to the correct people, Wes's title would be removed and given to the correct people. It would pass to the Americans. That child was the true heir, the firstborn, *if* the child was a boy."

"Um, William says that you can tell your family about the news from the journal. Your title might be pulled, and you would be free," I said, relaying the ghost's words. "Although that's what got William killed. He tried to do the same thing."

Wes stood abruptly. "I need to talk to my family. Thank you so much for sharing this journal with me." He gave me a quick hug and a kiss on the cheek.

There wasn't even time to process that Wes was leaving before he was gone.

William stared at me with sad eyes before also disappearing, but Maggie continued to stand next to me. She was just as confused as I was at Wes's reaction to my news.

Wasn't losing the title exactly what he had wanted?

CHAPTER FOURTEEN

Morning came early and with errands. There were last-minute touches to have the shop perfect for the Grand Re-Opening. Aunt Linda would be there already, and I didn't want to be a slacker.

Wes and his predicament weighed heavily on my mind as I drove into town. I shot him a text as soon as I parked.

Would you like me to grab something from the Deli for you? Otto makes great subs.

While I waited to hear from Wes, I threw myself into the work at the shop.

"How did things go with the ghost

last night?" Aunt Linda questioned as she carefully placed price stickers on the shelves.

Shooting her a wry grin, I only paused my straightening for a moment. "Well, Wes now knows I talk to ghosts. He came over to look at the journal." I filled her in on the rest of the conversation and what the ghost thought was a solution to righting the wrongs of their ancestor.

"What are you going to do about the love triangle you've found yourself in?" She wiggled her eyebrows. "Hmm? Dashing Deputy Don and Woo Woo Wes, the Viscount Vet?"

I laughed at the thought. "Woo Woo?"

"Gotta stick to alliteration. That's how the greats do it," she said with a chuckle at her attempt at humor.

Waving the feather duster at her, I set her straight. "Nah, it's not a love triangle. I'm too busy trying to solve murders with ghosts to worry about my love life."

Aunt Linda raised an eyebrow and

jerked her head toward the door. "You might need to tell Don that. He's on his way in."

Sure enough, Dashing Deputy Don himself was making his way to the shop door with a vase of flowers.

Panic flooded me, but I didn't have time to hide as he stepped through the door, the cheery bell announcing his arrival.

"Congratulations!" He held out the vase to me as he looked around, taking in the work we'd done. "The place looks wonderful. Better than ever."

"You didn't have to bring these," I said, sniffing the fragrant aroma of the flowers as I set the vase near the register. "But they are absolutely lovely."

"Yes, I did." He smiled at me.

"The shop definitely needed some flowers to celebrate the reopening with," I said, quickly trying to make the gesture about the shop and not me. "Thank you."

"I just wanted to wish you luck on

your first day back." He pointed to his badge. "I've got to get back to work."

Darn. He really did look dashing in his uniform. Threading my arm through his, I walked him out to his cruiser.

He tipped his hat to me. "Have a good day."

"He's a cutie," Aunt Linda commented as I re-entered the shop. "You'd better jump on that. A lot of girls would kill to have a man in uniform personally delivering them gifts."

"Auntie, it's not like that." I bent to smell the flowers again. "Besides, I have unresolved things with Wes."

She snorted. "It most certainly *is* like that. Both men like you, and you'd better be careful, or you'll have to choose between two good men," she warned knowingly, making a triangle with her fingers.

I rolled my eyes and resumed working on the candle arrangements and straightening the shelves. She was right, but I didn't want to admit that to myself, much less to her.

My followers were going to want to see the shop now that it was finished. I took a few videos of the inside and outside, talking about all the work we'd done, and giving proper credit to Aunt Linda, before seating myself in the back. It would take a few minutes to edit them before posting.

I'd just sent another text to Wes about lunch when the bell over the door chimed again.

"Are you the shop's owners?" an older woman asked with a younger companion in tow.

"Yes, we are." Aunt Linda smiled and moved to help the two ladies with their purchases.

"It's such a gorgeous place," the other one gushed as they each picked out candles in a variety of colors.

Those two led to others, and before long we had a near-constant stream of people stopping by to check the new setup and buy a few things. It was so busy that I couldn't check my phone or finish my video edits until it was almost lunchtime.

Nothing from Wes. He hadn't responded at all.

I frowned. "Auntie, I'm going to grab lunch." I stepped into the back to give Wes a call while she took over ringing up the customers.

On the second ring, he answered. "Hey, I've taken the day off. I'm still reading through the journal. This afternoon, I'm picking up my brother from the airport." The poor guy sounded frazzled and apologetic.

"How are you doing with it all?" I didn't want to push, but I was dying to know what he thought.

"It's a lot to take in and process. I want to be successful and finish what the William guy started." He chuckled. "This ghost guy is serious about letting me know he's here. He's been slamming doors and moving stuff all day."

He went silent for a second, then came back and spoke hurriedly. "Look, I have to go, but thanks for reaching out. I'll get back to you later. Bye." He hung up, and I was left staring at the phone in my hand.

Unsure of what to do, I noticed Maggie in the doorway. "Can I help you?" I asked kindly.

Maggie wrinkled her nose at me.

With a sigh, I let my shoulders slump. "I'm really sorry for the delay in helping you move on. I don't know what else to do. Kim is behind bars. I'm safe now, right?"

She shook her head no. Sadness filled her features before she disappeared.

CHAPTER FIFTEEN

Two days had passed since the shop's grand reopening and business had been steady. Things outside of the shop had been uneventful, but sadly, my texts to Wes had still gone unanswered, and I didn't want to bother him with another phone call. While I wanted to check on him, I decided I needed to focus on helping Maggie move on.

"I think we should go back over to the house and finish going through stuff," I suggested while we locked up the shop. "Maybe we'll find another clue about Maggie."

Linda pursed her lips, then nodded decisively. “Agreed. We can grab dinner and then spend the rest of the evening going through things.” Aunt Linda nodded again, pleased with the idea, but paused at her car. “We’re going to have to decide what to do with the house soon. The insurance will get back to me with an estimate of what they’ll cover. We’ll have to figure out if there will be enough to tear it down and have a new one built.”

We spent our evening covered in dust while going through most of the boxes. Several trips up the stairs to the attic later, I had most of it ready to be taken to a storage unit.

“Let’s leave the tunnels for another day.” Aunt Linda wiped sweat from her forehead when we got the last box into her car. “It’s late and hasn’t really been looked at yet. It can wait a few more days until we can really focus on it.”

“What should we do about the body that’s down there?” I scrunched up my face at the idea of disturbing it.

"That's up to Wes's family, really. We can't leave it down there, but where he needs to be buried is up to them." Aunt Linda brushed it off as she climbed in her car to head to storage. "I suppose we will need to notify the authorities at some point." She pulled out as I waved goodbye.

"Okay. Time to lock up and go home, I guess." I spoke to the empty air.

After securing the house as best I could, I headed home. Aunt Linda wasn't done at our storage building yet. Her car wasn't in our driveway. Though, Shadow waited for me on the porch. I let her inside only to find Maggie waiting for me.

"We went through the attic and there wasn't much to give us any answers on how to help you move on." I put my purse and keys on the entryway table. "Tomorrow, after work, I'll go down and check out the tunnels. I need some sleep right now."

Aunt Linda and I needed to finish work before we could look for more answers, but it had to be done and soon. We all needed some resolution.

It was late, so I didn't text Wes again. I should probably do that in the morning. If he didn't answer, as much as I hated it, I'd have to call him again if he kept ignoring my messages.

The next day was another early morning, and I dressed and headed into town. I'd slept pretty well, which was good as we were still busy.

I worked for several hours before deciding that I needed to take a break and visit with my shop friends. I didn't think I'd seen them since the ball.

Otto prepared lunch for Aunt Linda and me, but I knew coffee was urgent if I was going to survive the afternoon, so I headed to Jitterbug. While waiting for my usual coffee, Jitterbug's entrance swung open.

And in walked "Woo Woo Wes", as Aunt Linda had called him, and his brother. At least I assumed it was his brother. They looked nothing alike physically. His brother seemed cold, whereas

Wes had always given me the impression of being warm and welcoming. He was talking to Wes, but he didn't appear to be happy. The friendly vibes weren't there, and Wes looked especially uncomfortable.

Wes noticed me eyeing them and walked over. "Mags, this is my brother, William. He goes by Liam though."

I held out a hand as he introduced us. Interesting. Another William.

His grip was firm, but his touch sent bad vibes racing down my spine. I tried not to jerk my hand from his. It wouldn't do any good to be rude.

Liam moved toward me, but I stepped back, not wanting him in my space.

They didn't seem to have noticed my discomfort. "Liam is going to look at the journal while he's here," Wes announced.

"Where did you find it? It belongs to *our* family." Liam's tone was full of accusation as he interrupted his brother.

A look of panic must have crossed

my features as I looked at Wes for an answer.

He shook his head, confirming what I'd thought. He wasn't overly fond of his brother. "Nobody stole it, Liam. It was in her family's basement."

He notably hadn't mentioned the tunnels and made it seem like it was in a normal, run-of-the-mill basement. A rose by any other name, I suppose.

I shrugged. "We had a bunch of family things to go through down there, and I found it while I was sorting stuff." True enough.

"Maybe we should join you next time you sort things again?" Liam suggested. "In case there are any other pieces of our family history there."

I didn't mind Wes coming along but wasn't overly fond of Liam. "I was planning to go down there tonight."

William, the ghost, stood just behind Wes and shook his head, vehemently opposed to the idea.

Great, the ghost didn't like the idea. I

made a face at him before looking at Wes. "Can we talk for just a minute?" I motioned to the side of the seating area, out of Liam's hearing.

Liam got the hint and shot me a derisive look. "I'll just grab the coffee, Wes." He moved to the counter to give us privacy.

I spoke in a hushed whisper. "William is here, and he does not like the idea of you both looking through the tunnels."

"We won't be doing that with you there," Wes reassured me.

Though, if either of them thought they'd be going down there without me, they had another thing coming. "But you're going to have to decide what to do with William's body," I hissed. "It can't just stay down there forever. Beneath the house." I frowned at the horrible idea.

"I'll mention it to my family today. I'll need to find out how they want to handle it." Wes continued to face me but directed his words to William and the empty space next to me. "What would you like to happen to your remains?" he whispered.

"Home. I'd like to go home." William nodded and closed his eyes for a moment, seeming happy with the thought.

I relayed his response. "He wants to go home to England."

Liam came back holding both coffees. "When should we come over to check out that basement with you?" he pressed.

William shook his head once again.

I spread my hands out as if I were uncertain. "I'll have to let you know. It really depends on how the afternoon goes and if I need to go back down there with Aunt Linda. She has to give her permission."

"Very well. We'll be waiting for your message." Liam's frustration at my answer was quite apparent in the flare of his nostril and the set of his jaw. Wes had gotten all the good humor and charm.

"Yeah, we'd better let you get back to work." Wes ushered his brother out the door before I could respond.

Geez. Those two were brothers? Not such a happy family.

CHAPTER SIXTEEN

It was swap day, which meant I got to be the one to stay put in the shop for the afternoon while Aunt Linda ran the errands.

To my delight and confusion about how I felt about him, Don stopped by unexpectedly.

"Hey there," I said in a warm voice. "Come sit. I've got extra lunch if you want to join me." Otto had loaded me up, as usual. If Don didn't help me eat, it would become leftovers.

With a smile, he took a seat next to me. "How are things going with the reopening?" He dug into the lunch eagerly. "I haven't had a chance to stop by since just before you two officially went back into business."

I chewed a big bite of turkey before replying. "Everything has been so busy. We've run out of several items. What's even crazier is that social media and the videos I'm making are causing the online orders to skyrocket." I took a couple of bites. "Kind of wild, huh?"

"Yeah," he agreed. "Good wild."

Don stood after we'd shot the breeze about local happenings for a while after eating. I'd had to stop and help customers several times during the process.

"Well," he said. "I'd better be getting back to it."

He hadn't been gone long when Maggie appeared, her ghostly form reminding me that she was still with us.

"Tonight we'll get some answers," I promised.

She nodded, looking weary with me, and disappeared.

Aunt Linda returned before closing

time and looked around the rear stockroom with a pleased but surprised look on her face.

I sighed and put my hands on my hips. "Things are going to need to be restocked before this weekend. We won't have enough to fill all the walk-in customer orders along with the online orders."

"I've been thinking about that, Mags. What if you did certain scents that were available online only? Then we wouldn't be spread as thin. Some of our walk-in customers would go online to get the exclusive scents." She began to straighten up the shop so we could head home.

"Sounds wonderful." I started doing the same thing, neatening and tidying. "Maggie was here again. I promised that we'd check out the tunnels tonight. There's just one minor problem."

Her head jerked up, and she eyed me with concern. "What's that?"

"I met Wes's brother today in the coffee shop. Liam. William the ghost appeared, but he didn't want me to show them the tunnels. He said it was a bad idea."

She furrowed her brow. "Why would William care if you showed them the tunnels?"

"He didn't say. Just that he didn't want me to take them down there." I shrugged. "They'll have to go down there eventually to get William's body."

"If it's exhumed properly, then a professional will be the one that goes down there and not one of us or them. They'll know how to ship it back to England, so it won't get stuck in customs." She tapped her chin. "We'll insist on proper handling."

"Did you ever think that you'd be having a conversation about a body being exhumed from hidden tunnels in your house?" I laughed and held the door open as she grabbed her purse.

We both headed over to her house. I parked behind her, and we got out to go inside.

"The insurance called today," she said as she unlocked the door. "I'm just going to demolish the house. The inspector doesn't think it needs to be repaired but torn down instead." Aunt Linda sighed as we walked toward the tunnels. "It's too far gone."

"Will you build the same house again? Or is there something else that you want to do this time?" I looked at the molding and wondered how much could be salvaged for the new place.

She paused when we reached the top of the stairs. "The old house was where I'd always assumed that I'd grow old. Now, I'm not sure what I want to do." She flipped on the flashlight before going down.

Both of us aimed the flashlights into the darkness and toward the alcoves. There were antiques in several of them. "Here we go," I muttered.

The first one held a trunk and a table. I opened the trunk and found some linens that hadn't fared very well. Everything had aged and was falling apart.

The next alcove held a rocker, a

candlestick, and some busted wood. Nothing to explore, really, though I was dying to know some of the values of these pieces. Where was one of those Antique Roadshow guys when you needed them? I probably should've been filming some of this.

Wooden crates and chests filled the next space, but when I tried to open some of them, William appeared.

A gasp escaped from me. I guess some ghosts still managed to spook me. "Can I help you?" I asked, putting a hand over my still racing heart to help calm down.

"I sensed someone getting close to my body," he replied, his voice sorrowful.

"How are you holding up?" I scanned the floor with the flashlight so that I didn't step on his buried corpse. I had no idea where exactly it was, but it was apparently close enough to send William out.

"Wes needs to be protected," he stated, pacing the floor. "Other than that, I'm not entirely sure why I'm still here. I'm ready to be at peace. After all this time, I feel like it's well earned."

"That's what we're doing down here. I'm searching for something that will give you and Maggie some peace. There has to be something here, and I will not give up on you two."

I tried again in vain to open a crate. "Maybe Wes can do something with the information in the journal that will let you rest," I offered hopefully.

"That seems very unlikely," he said with a frown before disappearing as easily and with as little warning as when he'd appeared.

Aunt Linda came into the alcove where I stood.

"William was here," I said.

"I heard you talking to him." She shook her head. "Ghosts…"

The crates were stubborn and wouldn't let us open them without a crowbar. "We might as well leave them for tonight. I'm tired, and we have an early day at the shop again tomorrow."

Aunt Linda motioned for us to head back up the stairs.

Disappointed, but knowing she was right, I followed her as we called it a night.

CHAPTER SEVENTEEN

A few days later, I ran over to the Jitterbug to meet up with the other shop owners and Lucy.

"You guys did such an amazing job. Those new scents are to die for," Lacy raved. "I can't believe all the improvements you've made in the shop."

I couldn't stop my grin. "It's been so crazy. I mean, that's a good thing, really. We're going to have to restock again though." I sighed and took a sip of the coffee that Laura handed me. "Third time since we reopened. I've been making candles nonstop the last few days while Linda handles customers." We really needed another assistant. One that wouldn't try to kill us. Or burn the place down.

"How are you guys doing with prepping for the holiday rush?" I asked them.

"Well, there will be a rush of orders for dinner parties, but it's a lot of work." Otto nodded with experience.

"I always love all the lights and decorations, but I'm also glad when it's over." Laura sighed and took a seat at the table with the rest of us.

"What are we reading today?" I asked.

The book club moments with the shop owners were always a breath of fresh air. The perspective I gained, not from the reading, but from my friends, always gave me something to think about.

When I walked back into the Colonial Candles an hour later, Aunt Linda was rearranging another candle set. I hurried to help her get it just right.

"Maggie was here all morning." Aunt Linda frowned. "She was just watching."

"Ugh, I feel so guilty. I should have solved this thing for Maggie." I moved a couple of things just a smidge to complete the arrangement. "I don't think there are any bones or even a body left for us to find. We've discovered her murderer and Kim got arrested. I'm not sure there's anything I can do to help her move on at this point."

"We have to be missing something," Aunt Linda chimed in. "Why don't you run to the hardware store and pick up a crowbar? Then we'll be able to get those boxes open tonight. Maybe it will get us closer to helping Maggie move on."

"William mentioned at the ball that he was trying to protect Wes. Then I asked Maggie if she was here to protect me, and she nodded."

"If Kim is in jail and they found her guilty, what more do you need protected from?" Aunt Linda tilted her head at me.

"Couldn't agree more," I said, but I couldn't help but be nervous about what they could've been predicting.

After closing, armed with safety

glasses and a crowbar, we headed downstairs, ready to take on our mission. I set down a lantern I'd picked up at the hardware store when I got the crowbars. Much better than just the flashlights.

We arrived at the first crate that needed to be opened, only to stare at it.

"Do we even know how to use the crowbar?" We exchanged glances and burst out laughing.

I shrugged. "It seems a little self-explanatory, but I'm not sure where to start." I studied first one end and then the other. "Which one should I use?"

Linda laughed with me. "Only way to find out is to try."

A few minutes later, with no progress, I wasn't sure what to do. "We could always call the fire chief. He's been coming into the store a lot lately. Maybe he'd come help us."

"Aunt Linda." My voice rose two octaves as if I was scandalized. "When did *this* start?"

"He's been coming around a bit." She blushed, noticeable even in the electric lantern light. "He's brought lunch over a few times too."

I laughed at the way she was trying to downplay his attention. "There's always Wes. His brother wanted to come down anyway, and I'm sure they can help us."

"Would you be okay with that? Because you didn't feel right about it at first. What about Don?" She stood back, waiting for my answer.

"Um, yeah, I don't think that's a good idea either." I grimaced. He'd been texting me off and on all week.

Aunt Linda let out a huff and flapped her hand at me. "I'll order dinner and go get it. You call Wes and invite him down. Try to give him the hint that we only want *him*. He can open everything. Then while he's here, he can decide what to do with his ancestor's body."

"Ugh, I guess that is the best plan for tonight. I'll call him." I groaned and pulled out my phone.

I was surprised I had service, but it

rang easily, and he picked up on the second ring. "Wes?" His voice didn't sound right.

"No, this is Liam." Ugh. That was why.

"Oh, hello. Can I speak to Wes please?" I didn't want to be rude, but I wanted to speak to the less scary brother.

"He's with the last patient of the evening. Can I deliver a message for you?" Liam's suave tone made me feel icky.

"Um, sure. I was going through the tunnels and there were some crates we couldn't get open. I could use some help with those." I gasped as the words escaped before I could get them back. Scotch Bonnet.

"We can probably come help with that in about half an hour." Darn it. I should've lied. Double Scotch Bonnet.

"Thank you. I'll be outside to meet you." After hanging up, I went to find Aunt Linda leaning against her car.

"The food should be ready in about forty-five minutes," she announced. "I'll leave in about twenty so it will still be hot or as hot as it can be when I get back. We can bring up a few of those smaller things and put them on the backseat until later."

"Works for me." I followed her back downstairs for a load of the things we'd found while I waited on my helpers to arrive.

CHAPTER EIGHTEEN

Wes and his brother, Liam, arrived shortly after Aunt Linda went to town to get the food for everyone.

The ghostly form of William appeared right as the two exited their car. He followed closely behind them, shaking his head in disapproval.

I spared a glance to William, hoping for an answer, but quickly turned back to Wes and Liam. "Hey, thanks for coming to help us." I couldn't really speak to William in front of Liam.

"No, thank you for calling us," Liam said with a sickly-sweet smile.

I risked another glance at William.

"You are doing us a real service. Aunt Linda and I aren't strong enough to open a single box with the crowbar. The chests weren't that difficult, but the crates have old hand-forged nails. They don't make things like they used to, that's for sure."

"We can handle it." Liam spoke with confidence.

"Aunt Linda just left to go get some food for everyone. We can work on opening a few crates until she gets back. What do you think?"

"That was very thoughtful. I'll have to remember to thank her." Liam threw the words over his shoulder as he walked ahead of us into the house.

"It's the least we could do to thank you," I blurted to Wes. "I know we couldn't have attempted this on our own." I wished we'd been strong enough. I didn't mind Wes being here at all, but Liam…

"Liam, you'll want to take a right." I followed him as Wes kept up with me.

"You never knew about the doorway until you found the blueprints?" Liam's questions held a hint of suspicion. "This is all so insane."

"Never knew," I said.

"Unbelievable," he muttered under his breath.

We moved down the stairs and into the tunnels.

"I forgot my flashlight. Keep going toward the first alcove on the right. That's where the crates are located. I'll be right back." I hurried up the stairs and out of hearing range.

"William," I called quietly. "Come here."

He appeared, but it looked like it was difficult. His face turned taut and haggard. "I can't sustain this distance from my body or Wes for long." He struggled to stay there.

"Why are you so against them coming?"

"I can't see the future, but I just feel that it's a terrible idea." He blinked away.

The guys were talking loudly, and I hurried back down to join them.

William stood between Wes and Liam, watching them work on the first crate.

I shined my flashlight on the crate, and Wes looked up at me with a grin.

My return smile faded when I saw Maggie there, too.

The crate must have something important if both ghosts looked horrified watching it open.

Liam pulled off the top with a deafening squeal of the nails and stepped to the side with the lid.

I stepped forward. Everything inside was in much better condition than the other things left in the tunnel.

A hodgepodge of stuff greeted us. From old toys to cookbooks, to other handwritten documents. I glanced through them before passing them over to Wes and Liam.

"Do any of these have something to do with our family?" Liam scowled at the rattle in his hand.

"Not that I can see. They are all labeled as items from my family." There were several handwritten notes outlining who the items had belonged to. "There *could* be something since it was buried here with your ancestor."

William spoke up from behind them. "There won't be. I was just here to speak to a family member. I was in the tunnel because it was a place to escape my brother's attempt to kill me."

"Why was the journal in the tunnels to begin with?" Liam glanced around, making no attempt to hide his disgust. "Wes said you turned over the paperwork on Howe. It's odd that our families are tied together."

"It's more likely that our family just found the journal somewhere." I didn't want to tell him the truth. "I haven't seen anything that ties them together besides the body and the journal."

"That's a pretty big tie-in." He shook his head in disbelief.

If I could tell him the truth, he wouldn't believe it anyway, so I turned to the next crate. He'd have to remain suspicious.

CHAPTER NINETEEN

"What do you know about how William died?" Liam questioned me, his voice harsher than before.

I didn't want to tell him, and William stood there beside him, urging me to be quiet.

A confused expression crossed my face as I tried to buy some time. It just occurred to me that I didn't know precisely where William's body was. How would I explain to Liam *how* I knew the body was here? The grave would be undisturbed.

"Wes mentioned he thought the viscount knew a way around the title and inheritance but hasn't revealed the plan to me." He stared at Wes pointedly.

"I don't want the title or the estate." Wes bit his lip to keep from saying too much. "I'd like to stay here in this town and settle down." It was curious that Wes had brought his brother to town but hadn't told him the plan.

Wes gave his brother a withering look. "William was coming here to make things right, but then he died before he could. The journals are the road map to answering all the questions you have, Liam."

"I've read those journals. He was coming to rat out the General for his marital indiscretions. It's such a stupid plan." Liam scoffed and rolled his eyes.

"He was trying to get out of inheriting the title in the same way I want to," Wes declared. "Since it can't be passed, he was trying to have it revert back to the American's family."

"Is that even possible? Could they fight for the title?" Liam considered the options, looking none too happy about it.

William stood there wide-eyed, and Maggie stood beside him, looking equally stressed. She kept her focus on William, as if he could speak for her.

"Don't tell him. Stop this conversation." William sounded desperate.

I glanced between all of them, confused about how to keep this from getting out of hand.

"It could be disputed and taken from the child who received it through his mother. The one born after the illegitimate son over here in America. The title can be given away and would have already if William's brother hadn't killed him here in the tunnels." Wes continued explaining, even though Liam was looking completely disgusted.

"What do you mean?" Liam spat.

"William was killed over this stupid title. His brother murdered him to take his place, but because William already had a son, the brother could only step in and raise him. He didn't get the title. This whole family has put more stock in a title than in the people who oversaw it.

It's destroyed the family time and again. Look at General Howe. He had the title, and he was a complete jerk. He thought it made him better."

Liam stepped into the alcove with the crowbar, lifting it as he gestured wildly. "It makes us better. It literally makes us nobility."

Wes looked back at his brother in disgust.

William yelled, "Grab Wes and run."

I gasped as Liam continued gesturing wildly.

"You are destined to follow in William's path. He was an idiot," Liam yelled at Wes.

Wes didn't look intimidated by his brother at all. "Liam! That title should never have belonged to us. It was always theirs to begin with. The title can't be forfeited. I won't pass that burden on to my children."

"You've never respected the title and everything that was handed to you," Liam roared. "You're ungrateful and unworthy of the title."

Wes nodded. "That's what I'm saying. I shouldn't have the title. *None* of us should!"

"That title will be given to that illegitimate heir over my dead body. It should have been mine. You didn't deserve it." Liam lost it, swinging the crowbar and hitting Wes on the side of the head.

I screamed and took a step backward into the alcove as Liam stood over Wes. "Go get help," I whispered to William and Maggie. "Aunt Linda."

Liam couldn't hear what I said but stepped toward me angrily. "Shut up."

"How can I explain Wes and his girlfriend's deaths in the tunnels?" He paced at the entrance of the alcove, trapping me inside. "It could be a domestic dispute. Her house just burned. *She* could be the psycho."

He muttered aloud ideas, and each one just got worse and worse. "Maybe I could light the tunnels on fire and burn the whole thing down."

William blinked back into the tunnel.

"I tried. She's too far away. Maggie

stayed with Linda to express the need to hurry."

Liam was still pacing and muttering, and I glanced toward Wes. He lay crumpled on the dirty floor, and the wound on his head was bleeding heavily.

I wanted to move over to him, but I was certain that Liam would hurt me if I attempted to do so.

"Should I say anything? If I did, what would I say?" He continued muttering about the best way to get rid of us and make it look like we'd fought.

With a sharp look at me, he frowned. "Linda." He tapped the crowbar in his hand. "She'll be on her way back now. I have no time. Something has got to be done."

"It's a long way to the restaurant," I piped up. "She shouldn't be on her way back yet."

"I'm truly sorry you got involved in this. Sometimes things must be done for the greater good. This is that type of thing, unfortunately." He smiled grimly. "Stay put."

He marched to the other alcove, and I dove to Wes's side.

Noises sounded throughout the alcoves, echoing off the walls. Liam was moving things around. Crates were being opened until Liam said, "Thank God."

I put my finger to Wes' neck to check for his pulse. He was still alive. Blood covered my hands, and I knew I needed to put pressure on the wound to stop the bleeding. What if I put too much pressure and hurt him instead? Why hadn't I taken those first aid courses the hospital offered?

Fear clutched my throat and stopped me in my tracks as Liam came back toward me. I went hot and then cold. The sound of water spraying was ominous enough until the smell of oil reached me. He was going to burn the tunnels. There were wooden beams here and there helping support these alcoves.

Panic coursed through me. My heart pounded. I couldn't lift Wes to carry him out of a fire. I also didn't want to leave him.

"William, what do I do?" I groaned in despair.

The ghost flickered back and forth from one side of the tunnel to the other. "I will try to keep the smoke out of the alcove, but I can't do that and go to Linda. I won't have enough strength for both."

"Stay, and I'll try to keep Wes alive. If you can, keep both of us alive."

"Sorry," Liam called one more time as light came around the corner of the tunnel. "I have to do this."

The door scraped shut, and I pulled my sweater off to lightly put pressure on Wes's head. "I'm trying to be careful and not hurt you."

Smoke filled the tunnels, but William had managed to put a bubble around us. Very little smoke was coming into this alcove, and the fire hadn't reached us yet.

Along the edges, I could see it spreading to the other alcoves slowly. It was getting harder to breathe. More smoke was slipping in.

"I am sorry. I'm not able to keep it all out," William apologized.

"Thank you for what you're doing." I looked down at Wes to be sure he was still breathing.

"Did I choose the wrong plan? Should I have tried to pull him out?" I was second-guessing myself. The fire was over the front door now. Even if I had the strength, I wouldn't be able to move him now.

"You would not have been able to get him up the stairs by yourself before the fire overtook you," William reassured me.

My ears perked up as I heard my name being called by male voices.

"Someone is coming from the other side of the tunnels." William smiled at me. "Hold tight."

"Is there another entrance to the tunnels?" I crouched next to Wes, waiting to be rescued, as close to the floor as I could get without lying prostrate.

"Not that I know of." William shook

his head. "I never made it further than the alcove where I died."

"Mags," the voice called out again, but it was much closer this time.

"Here. We're in here," I yelled out, realizing that it was Don.

Don came through the smoke with another man about his size, in a matching uniform.

A cough escaped me, and I let out a relieved breath.

"Linda called us," Don informed me. "The remainder of the house is on fire, and the tunnels are full of smoke as well."

Don pulled me up and looked down at Wes.

"His brother, Liam, hit him in the head with a crowbar," I explained. "He's hurt really badly."

Don's eyes widened at the amount of blood pooling under Wes's head.

"Grab her," the other man ordered. "I'll get him."

"I can walk," I coughed out. "You have to be careful and get Wes out."

Don looked like he wanted to protest, but he joined the other officer.

"The fire and smoke have spread everywhere. I'll do my best to get you out," William promised as we left the alcove.

We went right, leading further into the tunnels, and we had to dodge bursts of flame coming from the wooden beams. One crashed down in front of us, blocking the path and forcing us to stop.

Don blurted out a cuss word.

"Scotch Bonnet! What do we do now?" I asked. We all looked around, trying to find a way out.

Maggie appeared and gestured for us to follow her.

"This way," I yelled to Don and turned to see where Maggie wanted us to go. I'd explain away how I knew where to go later. After a couple of turns, an exit appeared just ahead.

Smoke poured out behind us as we made our way out of the tunnel and into the woods behind the house before stopping to gasp for breath.

"Over here." Don waved then called EMS over the radio on his shoulder to come find us.

I turned to look at Wes. He had gone clammy, and he'd lost all color. "Is he alive?"

Don reached down to check his pulse. He nodded but grimaced as sirens filled the air. "Barely."

"Come on, come on," I muttered.

Don stepped away from Wes to look me over.

Covered in ash and soot, I was a dirty, bloody mess. "I'm fine. Nothing serious, but a few bruises."

The ambulance pulled up and the paramedics came running through the brush with a stretcher.

"She'll need to be looked at and treated for smoke inhalation, but him first." Don directed the EMS, and they hurried to try to save Wes.

CHAPTER TWENTY

Aunt Linda rushed into the hospital room.

They'd insisted that I ride with Wes to be checked out at the hospital, then someone had attached oxygen to my nose, but it didn't stop my auntie from hugging me tightly.

Don came in a few seconds after. He gave me an encouraging smile. "Hey, you're looking a little better."

Dang. I must've looked rough before, because there was a mirror over the sink in the corner and I was a *fright* right now.

"What happened down there?" Linda asked.

I shook my head and shrugged. "We were right about Wes's brother."

Aunt Linda looked panicked, but her worry turned to anger as I told them all about Liam.

I took a shuddering breath. "He hit Wes over the head and then found some lamp oil to start the fire before he left us there to die."

Aunt Linda turned to look at Don with wide eyes. "Are you going to do something?"

Don held up his hands. "I'll have someone come take a statement, but I've got to get a warrant started. We'll need officers out looking for Liam." He placed a gentle kiss on my cheek. "I'll be back." Then Don fled the room to begin the search.

Tears filled my eyes once it was just me and Auntie Linda.

Aunt Linda wrapped her arms around me again. "I've never been so scared in my life. When Maggie showed up with William, I knew something was wrong. William could barely talk, and I had to rely on Maggie's signals about the tunnels and to get help." Aunt Linda held a hand over her heart. "I drove the rest of the way at illegal speeds. We shouldn't tell Don that, though."

I laughed at her words.

"When I saw the smoke, I called Don and Chief Oswald."

"How did you know about the other entrance to the tunnels?" I was curious because she hadn't mentioned it before.

"I tried to come down there, but it was so full of smoke and fire. It was Maggie that showed me where to go. Then I was able to tell Don how to find you." She winked at me. "Don got here before fire and rescue. He really does like you."

"Well, thank God he does. We wouldn't have made it much longer in all the smoke." I shook my head. "Liam was going to kill us both over that foolish title."

Aunt Linda squeezed my hand.

I glanced toward the door. "Have you heard anything about Wes?" I was eager to find out how he was. "William came back to me once, but all I could understand was surgery."

Aunt Linda frowned. "I haven't heard anything."

As I finished explaining everything that happened, a nurse came in to check on me.

"What are they going to do with my niece? Are they keeping her or sending her home?" she demanded of the poor woman.

"We're monitoring her for now. They ran a few tests, and when we get the results back, then I'll have an answer for you." She didn't respond to Aunt Linda's testy attitude. She was probably used to it. "The doctor will make that decision if you get to stay or go home."

"I'm not leaving the hospital until I know something about Wes," I said, unable to keep the tears at bay.

The nurse smiled in understanding.

"There isn't any news yet. He's still in surgery, but that means they're doing the best they can for him right now." She patted my leg. "I wish I could give you some good news. We'll know soon enough."

Officers arrived after a bit and took both of our statements.

"Don is working on finding Liam. You should both get some rest while you can. There will be an officer outside the door to keep you safe," the officer taking the statement reassured us.

It sounded like a good idea. My eyes were already halfway closed as he said the words, though I couldn't stop thinking about Wes. I also couldn't stop the exhaustion.

When the doctor came into the room, it felt like I'd just closed my eyes for a nap, but it had been several hours.

Aunt Linda stretched as she woke up, eager to hear what the doctor had to tell us.

"You are a lucky lady," the doctor

said, studying his tablet. "Everything looks wonderful for now. We're going to give you a round of antibiotics as a precautionary measure, but the nurse should be in to help you get ready. We want to leave you on oxygen for as long as possible to give your lungs a little extra boost before we send you home." The doctor smiled, as if this was the best news ever.

I had mixed feelings about toting an oxygen tank home with me. I hoped that wasn't what they meant. But whatever it took to get better.

The nurse brought in the discharge papers and gave me a big grin. "Wes is out of surgery. He did phenomenally and is now in the ICU."

"If he did so well, then why have they put him in the ICU? Doesn't that mean he's still in danger?" I chewed my bottom lip.

"It's common practice for someone with head injuries. He'll need some extensive care when he comes out of the anesthesia. He was treated quickly, so that's in his favor. If there isn't any brain swelling or cranial bleeding, then he should be fine. It's looking good."

"Was there brain damage?" I latched on to the idea, already worrying about the worst-case scenario. "Is there a risk for that?"

"I'm not a doctor, so I can't say for sure. It wasn't something the doctors appeared concerned with. They acted like his outcome was a good one."

I threw back the covers. "Thank you. Is there any way I can see him?"

"The doctor is speaking to his family now. I'll finish up your discharge papers, but you should go home and rest. Then you can come up here tomorrow and see him." The nurse smiled as she got things ready for my release. "He should be awake by then, and you'll be feeling a little better."

I fretted about him being up here. "I don't want him to wake up alone."

"Oh, he's not alone. His brother is waiting there with him."

"What? That's the man that tried to kill him!" I yelled.

The nurse's eyes widened, and she took off running.

"Call Don. He needs to know." I motioned for Aunt Linda to get her phone because I had no idea where mine was.

Instead, she handed me the phone. I'd memorized Don's cell number in case I needed it. Not because I was his girlfriend or anything.

"Don," I tried not to yell into the phone as I put it on speaker. "Liam is in the hospital. The nurse said Wes' brother is visiting him. He's trying to finish the job."

"I'll make sure we get him. Gotta go." He hung up, and I breathed a sigh of relief.

"Auntie, I need to go up there. I can't just sit here all day not knowing if Wes is safe." I slid out of bed and pulled on the scrubs the nurse had brought for me to wear home.

Her phone rang before I got them fully on, and I picked it up.

"We've arrested him. Wes is safe. You're safe now, too." Don's triumphant words filled me with hope.

"Really?" I held my breath, hoping it was true.

"He's in handcuffs, and they're escorting him to the station now. The only reason there wasn't an officer on Wes's door is that the hospital got their wires crossed and didn't notify us that he'd been moved from recovery to a room."

"Oh, thank goodness. Thank you, Don." I held back the sobs of joy I could feel trying to escape.

His voice softened. "How are you? Are you going to be all right?"

"I'm filling out the discharge papers right now. They're giving me an inhaler and meds. They want to make sure that I'll stay as good as new, thanks to you anyway."

"Anytime. Can't have you dying on me, can I?"

"Nope." I smiled.

"I'll let you go home. I'll check on you tomorrow." The line clicked.

"What happens now?" I asked Aunt Linda, unsure if we should go home.

"Let's rest for the night and come back tomorrow. Then you can look at Wes all you need to." She smiled as if she knew I'd do it no matter what.

When we arrived the next day, they wouldn't let more than one person in the room at a time.

I sat on the edge of the bed while Aunt Linda stood just outside the door, meaning we were *technically* obeying the rules.

"How do we get William and Maggie to cross over? Isn't their job done now?" I asked her through the doorway. Wes was still sound asleep. The nurses said he might be out for hours more as his body recovered from the ordeal he'd been through.

Shadow jumped up on the bed with a soft purr.

"What are you doing here? They

don't allow animals in the hospital," I whispered.

She just meowed and looked up at me. Then she put her paw on my knee.

We both laughed at her antics.

A moment later, Maggie appeared next to Wes's bed, looking more at peace.

"Thank you so much for helping to save me," I said, wishing I could hug her or squeeze her hand or something to tell her thank you.

She gave us a soft smile and disappeared.

Somehow, I knew that was it. She'd found her peace. William stared at the spot where Maggie had stood.

He frowned. "Unfair. When's it my turn?"

I chuckled as Wes opened his eyes. "I'm not sure exactly what we did to give Maggie her peace, but you're next, William. Don't worry. I know you'll find your way."

Ready for Mags's and Shadow's next great adventure?

PLEAS OF THE POLTERGEIST is now available.

CLICK HERE to get your copy so that you can keep reading this series today!

WHAT'S NEXT?

PLEAS OF THE POLTERGEIST is now available.

CLICK HERE to get your copy so that you can keep reading this series today!

MORE MOLLY

ABOUT MOLLY FITZ

While USA Today bestselling author Molly Fitz can't technically talk to animals, she and her doggie best friend, Sky Princess, have deep and very animated conversations as they navigate their days. Add to that, five more dogs, a snarky feline, comedian husband, and diva daughter, and you can pretty much imagine how life looks at the Casa de Fitz.

Molly lives in a house on a high hill in the Michigan woods and occasionally ventures out for good food, great coffee, or to meet new animal friends.

Writing her quirky, cozy animal mysteries is pretty much a dream come true, but sometimes she also goes by the names Melissa Storm and Mila Riggs and writes a very different kind of story.

Learn more, grab the free app, or sign up for her newsletter at **www.MollyMysteries.com**!

PET WHISPERER P.I.

Angie Russo just partnered up with Blueberry Bay's first ever talking cat detective. Along with his ragtag gang of human and animal helpers, Octo-Cat is determined to save the day… so long as it doesn't interfere with his schedule. Start with book 1, ***Kitty Confidential***.

PARANORMAL TEMP AGENCY

Tawny Bigford's simple life takes a turn for the magical when she stumbles upon her landlady's murder and is recruited by a talking black cat named Fluffikins to take over the deceased's role as the official Town Witch for Beech Grove, Georgia. Start with book 1, **Witch for Hire**.

MERLIN THE MAGICAL FLUFF

Gracie Springs is not a witch... but her cat is. Now she must help to keep his secret or risk spending the rest of her life in some magical prison. Too bad trouble seems to find them at every turn! Start with book 1, **Merlin the Magical Fluff.**

THE MEOWING MEDIUM (WITH L.A. BORUFF)

Mags McAllister lives a simple life making candles for tourists in historic Larkhaven, Georgia. But when a cat with mismatched eyes enters her life, she finds herself with the ability to see into the realm of spirits... Now the ghosts of people long dead have started coming to her for help solving their cold cases. Start with book 1, **Secrets of the Specter**.

THE PAINT-SLINGING SLEUTH (WITH LINNIE ROSE)

Following a freak electrical storm, Lisa Lewis's vibrant paintings of fairytale creatures have started coming to life. Unfortunately, only she can see and communicate with them. And when her mentor turns up dead, this aspiring artist must turn amateur sleuth to clear her name and save the day with only these "pigments" of her imagination to help her. Start with book 1, **My Colorful Conundrum**.

SPECIAL COLLECTIONS

Pet Whisperer P.I. Books 1-3
Pet Whisperer P.I. Books 4-6
Pet Whisperer P.I. Books 7-9
Pet Whisperer P.I. Books 10-12

CONNECT WITH MOLLY

You can download my free app here:

mollymysteries.com/app

Or sign up for my newsletter and get a special digital prize pack for joining, including an exclusive story, Meowy Christmas Mayhem, fun quiz, and lots of cat pictures!

mollymysteries.com/subscribe

Have you ever wanted to talk to animals? You can chat with Octo-Cat and help him solve an exclusive online mystery here:

mollymysteries.com/chat

Or maybe you'd like to chat with other animal-loving readers as well as to learn about new books and giveaways as soon as they happen! Come join Molly's VIP reader group on Facebook.

mollymysteries.com/group

MORE L.A.

ABOUT L.A. BORUFF

L.A. (Lainie) Boruff lives in East Tennessee with her husband, three children, and an ever growing number of cats. She loves reading, watching TV, and procrastinating by browsing Facebook. L.A.'s passions include vampires, food, and listening to heavy metal music. She once won a Harry Potter trivia contest based on the books and lost one based on the movies. She has two bands on her bucket list that she still hasn't seen: AC/DC and Alice Cooper. Feel free to send tickets.

Learn more or sign up for her newsletter at **www.laboruff.com**!

PRIMETIME OF LIFE

Turning forty isn't as exciting as most people think. There are no fireworks or sur-prise parties, and I definitely didn't get hitched overnight. Been there, got the di-vorce papers to prove it. Nope, none of that. Rather than forty being the new twenty and all that, I inherited a new power from my mysterious birth mother. But now she's dead and I, despite the fact that I have exactly zero training, I'm the next time-traveling assassin. Don't get excited. The job sounds glamorous, but it comes with a huge learning curve and plenty of mishaps. Then there's having to actually assassinate people. That part sucks. It could be worse. I could still be working retail.

WITCHING AFTER FORTY

Widow and empty nester, Ava Harper, never dreamed of turning forty without the love of her life. Nor did she know she would bury her favorite aunt, who raised her af-ter the death of her mother, a few years later. Then again, she doesn't have the power of foresight. No, her powers are much darker. Powers she has kept behind lock and key. With her only son off to college and her life savings depleted, Ava returns home to Shipton Harbor, Maine. She's only there to clean out, fix up, and sell the family home. But like everything in her life in the last five years, things change. Plans get canceled. Arriving in Shipton Harbor is like stepping into another world. Her high school rival is married to her best friend and is set on making up for every devious thing she did when they were teens. The magic in the house reawakens, making it impossible to sell. It doesn't want new owners, apparently. And to top it all, the sheriff looks like he belongs on the cover of a romance novel. When an old friend of the family turns up dead, Ava must delve deep into the powers she's repressed all her adult life to find the killer. Only a necromancer could've killed her friend. Now she must open up to her own wells of dark magic to find the murderer while working with the hottie sheriff she's sure has his own secrets.

MAGICAL MIDLIFE IN MYSTIC HOLLOW

No one ever told me what to do if I ended up forty-something, divorced, and job-less. When my ex knocks at my door with his new girlfriend I somehow manage to turn them into toads. But that's not possible, right? Still, my ex-husband's car is in the driveway, and he's nowhere to be found. Which doesn't look great for me. So I do the only rational thing I can think of… I run for it, straight back to the small town I grew up in. Mystic Hollow is exactly the way I remember it, except now it seems that every-thing I thought was normal and boring is supernatural. Even my group of childhood friends appear to be magical in unexpected ways. And the hot guy I had a schoolgirl crush on? Apparently, he's an alpha shifter who digs me. Moving back home might be the fun I've been missing. That is until my brother disappears. Now, it's up to me to find him, even if I have to take on vampires, shifters, sirens, and a whole lot of crazy to do it. I know that so long as I have my friends backing me, I'll find him because no one wants to be on karma's bad side...

THE MEOWING MEDIUM

Mags McAllister lives a simple life making candles for tourists in historic Larkhaven, Georgia. But when a cat with mismatched eyes enters her life, she finds herself with the ability to see into the realm of spirits... Now the ghosts of people long dead have started coming to her for help solving their cold cases.

FANGED AFTER FORTY

Jilted at the altar a month before her fortieth birthday. Poor Hailey. Midlife really does have a crisis. Or is it that midlife is the crisis? Either way, it sucks. Hailey Whitfield can't take anymore run-ins with her ex. It's time for a big change. She's never consid-ered moving away, but it's her best plan yet. Bonus – her bestie lives next door! How-ever, her new neighbor is… weird, to say the least. Extremely hot, but odd. So are his friends. But Hailey will take strange neighbors over facing her lying, cheat, deadbeat ex-fiancé all day, any day. Finding a job in a new town is more challenging than she realizes. With her savings depleted from the move, Hailey has to suck it up and take what she gets. After taking a job as a private nurse for an injured bounty hunter, things start to look up. Then a skip falls into her lap. Okay, sure. She was being nosy and reading an incoming fax intended for her patient. But with a little encouragement,

Hailey takes on the task of tracking down the skip. It's easy money. Right? Wrong. This skip is far more than Hailey bargained for. And her life is about to change in a very bloody and pointy kind of way. What a bite in the… Well, you know. With the help of her witchy best friend and her new, very pale neighbor, Hailey is going to collect her bounty. Or die trying.

MORE BOOKS LIKE THIS

Welcome to Whiskered Mysteries, where each and every one of our charming cozies comes with a furry sidekick... or several! Around here, you'll find we're all about crafting the ultimate reading experience. Whether that means laugh-out-loud antics, jaw-dropping magical exploits, or whimsical journeys through small seaside towns, you decide.

So go on and settle into your favorite comfy chair and grab one of our *paw*some cozy mysteries to kick off your next great reading adventure!

Visit our website to browse our books and meet our authors, to jump into our discussion group, or to join our newsletter. See you there!

www.WhiskeredMysteries.com

WHISKMYS (WĬSK'MƏS)

DEFINITION : a state of fiction-induced euphoria that commonly occurs in those who read books published by the small press, Whiskered Mysteries.

USAGE: Every day is Whiskmys when you have great books to read!

Made in the USA
Monee, IL
09 March 2022